AE. ENGRAVING

At first I thought it was a joke, just a silly song he sang to taunt me while I was shackled in his penthouse at the end of the world. After seeing his mind shattered, his body petrified, and his chaos reversed, I knew he _must_ be gone from our reality. And yet some mornings I wake up with a tune stuck in my head, and I curse when I realize what I'm whistling . . .

WE'LL MEET AGAIN...

The question continues to nag at me, like a thistle in my sock: <u>IS BILL CIPHER REALLY DEAD?</u> In the weeks since Weirdmageddon, I conducted numerous tests on Stanley's mind (his terrible jokes are still intact) and inspected the statue for dimensional leakage (we also took turns kicking the statue, and Stanley took a few cracks with a crowbar). I burned every Cipher-shaped item I had ever collected, and even threw away all my one-dollar bills, just to be safe (Stanley, of course, found and pocketed them).

But the Memory Gun's effects have proven to be far from permanent. If memories could return . . . I shudder to think what else could return as well . . .

I was recently packing for a long-overdue family trip when I found something nestled in my knapsack: a black book with a triangle on the cover. Dismissing it as a tasteless prank (some local teens think "Bill worship" is "edgy"), I threw the book in the trash, shot the trash with a shotgun, and hurled it all into a ravine.

IMPERMANENT?

But the book reappeared under my pillow the next morning, unscathed. And again the next. I have since tried burning, stabbing, tearing, freezing, and molecularly destabilizing this book, as well as feeding it to Mabel's pet pig, but it somehow always returns, haunting me. I have told none about it, not wanting to alarm them, because I know what this is. I've heard the myths but didn't want to believe they were true. This really is **THE BOOK OF BILL**

Created by forces unknown, printed on stitched-together human brain matter, sealed with black wax, moonstones, and invisible symbols, his book has one purpose: to conjure Cipher's voice into its pages. To communicate with the Triangle . . . even after his death.

This is not an ordinary book. It appears differently to everyone, sometimes seeming completely empty, other times full of incomprehensible gibberish.

It changes and rewrites itself based on the mind of any reader with the misfortune of holding it. It will become whatever it must to deceive you, to pull you in. It's not safe on a bookshelf, because, as I have witnessed:

STAY BACK

IT INFECTS OTHER BOOKS

Why has it appeared now? I only have my suspicions. But my days of doing _his_ bidding are behind me. There are still small rifts to the Nightmare Realm that my family and I have been sealing as I repair the damage from Weirdmageddon. I am tossing this book into one of those rifts and not looking back.

If this book has somehow found its way to you, then you are the next target it has chosen. I offer a warning: destroy it. I tried to destroy it, heaven knows I tried, but every attempt proved futile. Whatever you do:

DO NOT TURN ITS PAGES.
DO NOT WRITE YOUR NAME.
DO NOT BELIEVE A WORD.

Turn back while you still can.
Or live forever with the regret.

STANFORD PINES

THIS BOOK'S NEW MASTER IS

X

_____

(YOUR NAME HERE)

To SUMMON

1) PLACE YOUR HAND ON THE RIGHT PAGE

2) CLEAR YOUR MIND

3) REPEAT THE WORDS

"TIME TO GET WEIRD"

AHAHAHAHAHAHAHAHAHAHAHAHAHAHAHAHAHAHAHAHAHAHAHAHAHA
HAHAHAHAHAHAHAHAHAHAHAHAHAHAHAHAHAHAHAHAHAHAHAHAHAH
AHAHAHAHAHAHAHAHAHAHAHAHAHAHAHAHAHAHAHAHAHAHAHAHAHA
HAHAHAHAHAHAHAHAHAHAHAHAHAHAHAHAHAHAHAHAHAHAHAHAHAH
AHAHAHAHAHAHAHAHAHAHAHAHAHAHAHAHAHAHAHAHAHAHAHAHAHA
HAHAHAHAHAHAHAHAHAHAHAHAHAHAHAHAHAHAHAHAHAHAHAHAHAH
AHAHAHAHAHAHAHAHAHAHAHAHAHAHAHAHAHAHAHAHAHAHAHAHAHA
HAHAHAHAHAHAHAHAHAHAHAHAHAHAHAHAHAHAHAHAHAHAHAHAHAH
AHAHAHAHAHAHAHAHAHAHAHAHAHAHAHAHAHAHAHAHAHAHAHAHAHA
HAHAHAHAHAHAHAHAHAHAHAHAHAHAHAHAHAHAHAHAHAHAHAHAHAI
AHAHAHAHAHAHAHAHAHAHAHAHAHAHAHAHAHAHAHAHAHAHAHAHAHA
HAHAHAHAHAHAHAHAHAHAHAHAHAHAHAHAHAHAHAHAHAHAHAHAHAH
AHAHAHAHAHAHAHAHAHAHAHAHAHAHAHAHAHAHAHAHAHAHAHAHAHA
HAHAHAHAHAHAHAHAHAHAHAHAHAHAHAHAHAHAHAHAHAHAHAHAHAH
AHAHAHAHAHAHAHAHAHAHAHAHAHAHAHAHAHAHAHAHAHAHAHAHAHA
HAHAHAHAHAHAHAHAHAHAHAHAHAHAHAHAHAHAHAHAHAHAHAHAHAH
AHAHAHAHAHAHAHAHAHAHAHAHAHAHAHAHAHAHAHAHAHAHAHAHAHA
HAHAHAHAHAHAHAHAHAHAHAHAHAHAHAHAHAHAHAHAHAHAHAHAHAH
AHAHAHAHAHAHAHAHAHAHAHAHAHAHAHAHAHAHAHAHAHAHAHAHAHA
HAHAHAHAHAHAHAHAHAHAHAHAHAHAHAHAHAHAHAHAHAHAHAHAHAH
AHAHAHAHAHAHAHAHAHAHAHAHAHAHAHAHAHAHAHAHAHAHAHAHAHA
HAHAHAHAHAHAHAHAHAHAHAHAHAHAHAHAHAHAHAHAHAHAHAHAHAH
AHAHAHAHAHAHAHAHAHAHAHAHAHAHAHAHAHAHAHAHAHAHAHAHAHA
HAHAHAHAHAHAHAHAHAHAHAHAHAHAHAHAHAHAHAHAHAHAHAHAHAH
AHAHAHAHAHAHAHAHAHAHAHAHAHAHAHAHAHAHAHAHAHAHAHAHAHA
HAHAHAHAHAHAHAHAHAHAHAHAHAHAHAHAHAHAHAHAHAHAHAHAHAF
AHAHAHAHAHAHAHAHAHAHAHAHAHAHAHAHAHAHAHAHAHAHAHAHAHA
HAHAHAHAHAHAHAHAHAHAHAHAHAHAHAHAHAHAHAHAHAHAHAHAHAF
AHAHAHAHAHAHAHAHAHAHAHAHAHAHAHAHAHAHAHAHAHAHAHAHAHA
HAHAHAHAHAHAHAHAHAHAHAHAHAHAHAHAHAHAHAHAHAHAHAHAHAF
AHAHAHAHAHAHAHAHAHAHAHAHAHAHAHAHAHAHAHAHAHAHAHAHAHA
HAHAHAHAHAHAHAHAHAHAHAHAHAHAHAHAHAHAHAHAHAHAHAHAHAF
AHAHAHAHAHAHAHAHAHAHAHAHAHAHAHAHAHAHAHAHAHAHAHAHAHA
HAHAHAHAHAHAHAHAHAHAHAHAHAHAHAHAHAHAHAHAHAHAHAHAHAF
AHAHAHAHAHAHAHAHAHAHAHAHAHAHAHAHAHAHAHAHAHAHAHAHAHA

AHAHAHAHAHAHAHAHAHAHAHAHAHAHAHAHAHAHAHAHAHAHAHAHAHAHAHAHAHAHAHA
HAHAHAHAHAHAHAHAHAHAHAHAHAHAHAHAHAHAHAHAHAHAHAHAHAHAHAHAHAHAHAH
AHAHAHAHAHAHAHAHAHAHAHAHAHAHAHAHAHAHAHAHAHAHAHAHAHAHAHAHAHAHAHA
HAHAHAHAHAHAHAHAHAHAHAHAHAHAHAHAHAHAHAHAHAHAHAHAHAHAHAHAHAHAHAH
AHAHAHAHAHAHAHAHAHAHAHAHAHAHAHAHAHAHAHAHAHAHAHAHAHAHAHAHAHAHAHA
HAHAHAHAHAHAHAHAHAHAHAHAHAHAHAHAHAHAHAHAHAHAHAHAHAHAHAHAHAHAHAH
AHAHAHAHAHAHAHAHAHAHAHAHAHAHAHAHAHAHAHAHAHAHAHAHAHAHAHAHAHAHAHA
HAHAHAHAHAHAHAHAHAHAHAHAHAHAHAHAHAHAHAHAHAHAHAHAHAHAHAHAHAHAHAH
AHAHAHAHAHAHAHAHAHAHAHAHAHAHAHAHAHAHAHAHAHAHAHAHAHAHAHAHAHAHAHA
HAHAHAHAHAHAHAHAHAHAHAHAHAHAHAHAHAHAHAHAHAHAHAHAHAHAHAHAHAHAHAH
AHAHAHAHAHAHAHAHAHAHAHAHAHAHAHAHAHAHAHAHAHAHAHAHAHAHAHAHAHAHAHA
HAHAHAHAHAHAHAHAHAHAHAHAHAHAHAHAHAHAHAHAHAHAHAHAHAHAHAHAHAHAHAH
AHAHAHAHAHAHAHAHAHAHAHAHAHAHAHAHAHAHAHAHAHAHAHAHAHAHAHAHAHAHAHA
HAHAHAHAHAHAHAHAHAHAHAHAHAHAHAHAHAHAHAHAHAHAHAHAHAHAHAHAHAHAHAH
AHAHAHAHAHAHAHAHAHAHAHAHAHAHAHAHAHAHAHAHAHAHAHAHAHAHAHAHAHAHAHA
HAHAHAHAHAHAHAHAHAHAHAHAHAHAHAHAHAHAHAHAHAHAHAHAHAHAHAHAHAHAHAH
AHAHAHAHAHAHAHAHAHAHAHAHAHAHAHAHAHAHAHAHAHAHAHAHAHAHAHAHAHAHAHA
HAHAHAHAHAHAHAHAHAHAHAHAHAHAHAHAHAHAHAHAHAHAHAHAHAHAHAHAHAHAHAH
AHAHAHAHAHAHAHAHAHAHAHAHAHAHAHAHAHAHAHAHAHAHAHAHAHAHAHAHAHAHAHA
HAHAHAHAHAHAHAHAHAHAHAHAHAHAHAHAHAHAHAHAHAHAHAHAHAHAHAHAHAHAHAH
AHAHAHAHAHAHAHAHAHAHAHAHAHAHAHAHAHAHAHAHAHAHAHAHAHAHAHAHAHAHAHA
HAHAHAHAHAHAHAHAHAHAHAHAHAHAHAHAHAHAHAHAHAHAHAHAHAHAHAHAHAHAHAH
AHAHAHAHAHAHAHAHAHAHAHAHAHAHAHAHAHAHAHAHAHAHAHAHAHAHAHAHAHAHAHA
HAHAHAHAHAHAHAHAHAHAHAHAHAHAHAHAHAHAHAHAHAHAHAHAHAHAHAHAHAHAHAH
AHAHAHAHAHAHAHAHAHAHAHAHAHAHAHAHAHAHAHAHAHAHAHAHAHAHAHAHAHAHAHA
HAHAHAHAHAHAHAHAHAHAHAHAHAHAHAHAHAHAHAHAHAHAHAHAHAHAHAHAHAHAHAH
AHAHAHAHAHAHAHAHAHAHAHAHAHAHAHAHAHAHAHAHAHAHAHAHAHAHAHAHAHAHAHA
HAHAHAHAHAHAHAHAHAHAHAHAHAHAHAHAHAHAHAHAHAHAHAHAHAHAHAHAHAHAHAH
AHAHAHAHAHAHAHAHAHAHAHAHAHAHAHAHAHAHAHAHAHAHAHAHAHAHAHAHAHAHAHA
HAHAHAHAHAHAHAHAHAHAHAHAHAHAHAHAHAHAHAHAHAHAHAHAHAHAHAHAHAHAHAH
AHAHAHAHAHAHAHAHAHAHAHAHAHAHAHAHAHAHAHAHAHAHAHAHAHAHAHAHAHAHAHA
HAHAHAHAHAHAHAHAHAHAHAHAHAHAHAHAHAHAHAHAHAHAHAHAHAHAHAHAHAHAHAH
AHAHAHAHAHAHAHAHAHAHAHAHAHAHAHAHAHAHAHAHAHAHAHAHAHAHAHAHAHAHAHA
HAHAHAHAHAHAHAHAHAHAHAHAHAHAHAHAHAHAHAHAHAHAHAHAHAHAHAHAHAHAHAH
AHAHAHAHAHAHAHAHAHAHAHAHAHAHAHAHAHAHAHAHAHAHAHAHAHAHAHAHAHAHAHA
HAHAHAHAHAHAHAHAHAHAHAHAHAHAHAHAHAHAHAHAHAHAHAHAHAHAHAHAHAHAHAH

HAHAHAHAHAHAHAHAHAHAHAHAHAHAHAHAHAHAHAHAHAHAHAHAHAHAHAHAHAHAHAHAH
AHAHAHAHAHAHAHAHAHAHAHAHAHAHAHAHAHAHAHAHAHAHAHAHAHAHAHAHAHAHAHAHA
HAHAHAHAHAHAHAHAHAHAHAHAHAHAHAHAHAHAHAHAHAHAHAHAHAHAHAHAHAHAHAHAH
AHAHAHAHAHAHAHAHAHAHAHAHAHAHAHAHAHAHAHAHAHAHAHAHAHAHAHAHAHAHAHAHA
HAHAHAHAHAHAHAHAHAHAHAHAHAHAHAHAHAHAHAHAHAHAHAHAHAHAHAHAHAHAHAHAF
AHAHAHAHAHAHAHAHAHAHAHAHAHAHAHAHAHAHAHAHAHAHAHAHAHAHAHAHAHAHAHAHA
HAHAHAHAHAHAHAHAHAHAHAHAHAHAHAHAHAHAHAHAHAHAHAHAHAHAHAHAHAHAHAHAF
AHAHAHAHAHAHAHAHAHAHAHAHAHAHAHAHAHAHAHAHAHAHAHAHAHAHAHAHAHAHAHAHA
HAHAHAHAHAHAHAHAHAHAHAHAHAHAHAHAHAHAHAHAHAHAHAHAHAHAHAHAHAHAHAHAF
AHAHAHAHAHAHAHAHAHAHAHAHAHAHAHAHAHAHAHAHAHAHAHAHAHAHAHAHAHAHAHAHA
HAHAHAHAHAHAHAHAHAHAHAHAHAHAHAHAHAHAHAHAHAHAHAHAHAHAHAHAHAHAHAHAF
AHAHAHAHAHAHAHAHAHAHAHAHAHAHAHAHAHAHAHAHAHAHAHAHAHAHAHAHAHAHAHAHA
HAHAHAHAHAHAHAHAHAHAHAHAHAHAHAHAHAHAHAHAHAHAHAHAHAHAHAHAHAHAHAHAF
AHAHAHAHAHAHAHAHAHAHAHAHAHAHAHAHAHAHAHAHAHAHAHAHAHAHAHAHAHAHAHAHA
HAHAHAHAHAHAHAHAHAHAHAHAHAHAHAHAHAHAHAHAHAHAHAHAHAHAHAHAHAHAHAHAF
AHAHAHAHAHAHAHAHAHAHAHAHAHAHAHAHAHAHAHAHAHAHAHAHAHAHAHAHAHAHAHAHA
HAHAHAHAHAHAHAHAHAHAHAHAHAHAHAHAHAHAHAHAHAHAHAHAHAHAHAHAHAHAHAHAF
AHAHAHAHAHAHAHAHAHAHAHAHAHAHAHAHAHAHAHAHAHAHAHAHAHAHAHAHAHAHAHAHA
HAHAHAHAHAHAHAHAHAHAHAHAHAHAHAHAHAHAHAHAHAHAHAHAHAHAHAHAHAHAHAHAH
AHAHAHAHAHAHAHAHAHAHAHAHAHAHAHAHAHAHAHAHAHAHAHAHAHAHAHAHAHAHAHAHA
HAHAHAHAHAHAHAHAHAHAHAHAHAHAHAHAHAHAHAHAHAHAHAHAHAHAHAHAHAHAHAHAH
AHAHAHAHAHAHAHAHAHAHAHAHAHAHAHAHAHAHAHAHAHAHAHAHAHAHAHAHAHAHAHAHA
HAHAHAHAHAHAHAHAHAHAHAHAHAHAHAHAHAHAHAHAHAHAHAHAHAHAHAHAHAHAHAHAH
AHAHAHAHAHAHAHAHAHAHAHAHAHAHAHAHAHAHAHAHAHAHAHAHAHAHAHAHAHAHAHAHA
HAHAHAHAHAHAHAHAHAHAHAHAHAHAHAHAHAHAHAHAHAHAHAHAHAHAHAHAHAHAHAHAH
AHAHAHAHAHAHAHAHAHAHAHAHAHAHAHAHAHAHAHAHAHAHAHAHAHAHAHAHAHAHAHAHA
HAHAHAHAHAHAHAHAHAHAHAHAHAHAHAHAHAHAHAHAHAHAHAHAHAHAHAHAHAHAHAHAH
AHAHAHAHAHAHAHAHAHAHAHAHAHAHAHAHAHAHAHAHAHAHAHAHAHAHAHAHAHAHAHAHA
HAHAHAHAHAHAHAHAHAHAHAHAHAHAHAHAHAHAHAHAHAHAHAHAHAHAHAHAHAHAHAHAH

WELL **WELL**

WELL

HERE WE ARE AT *LAST!*
I'VE BEEN WAITING AN *ETERNITY* TO MEET YOU, AND
I KNOW YOU'VE BEEN WAITING NEARLY AS LONG TO
MEET ME!
BREATHE IT IN A SECOND, PAL—THIS MOMENT OF
ANTICIPATION! YOU ALWAYS SUSPECTED THIS DAY
WOULD COME, AND IT FINALLY HAS! YOUR LIFE WILL
FOREVER BE DIVIDED INTO TWO HALVES:
BEFORE YOU MET ME, AND *AFTER.*

WELCOME TO THE AFTER.

YOU'RE PROBABLY WONDERING, "BILL, YOU'RE AN
ALL-POWERFUL BEING. WHY WRITE A BOOK, HUH?
WHY LET ME READ IT? **ALSO, AREN'T YOU DEAD? ARE YOU
DEAD OR WHAT? WHAT'S THE DEAL?"**

I HAVE NO IDEA WHAT YOU MEAN . . .

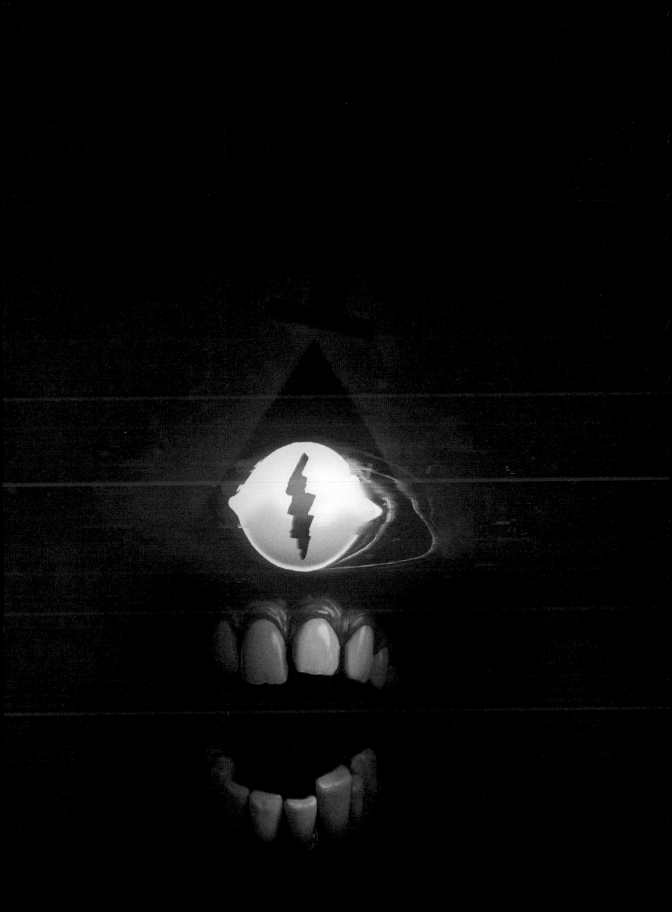

In fact, I'm better than fine, because now I have you! And there's a lot we can do together! Oh, you might feel silly about "meeting" me. After all, "Bill Cipher" is imaginary. You're real and I'm not, right?

BUT ARE YOU SO SURE ABOUT THAT?

After all, you're mortal. One day, you'll be dust. But I'm an idea. And an idea can't be killed. So that's me 1, you 0 on the immortality front! And if I'm the eternal one and you're the temporary one, THEN IT MIGHT BE WISE FOR YOU TO GET ON THE WINNING SIDE EARLY, YOU DIG?

I know that drama queen Sixer warned you not to read this book, didn't he? Maybe the old nerd is right! Weak minds have gone crazy from just ONE glimpse at my TANTALIZING FORBIDDEN SECRETS! (See: the hickory-smoked crater where McGucket's brain used to be!)

But if you're as sharp as I think you are . . . and if you're curious about the meaning of life, how to cheat death, Pine Tree's most embarrassing dreams, and your own interesting future, then I'll consider making a deal with you. How about a trade? I'll let you read my book in exchange for a favor down the line. We can work out the details later. What do you say?

TAKE BILL'S DEAL?

TURN THE PAGE

TURN TO PAGE 77

Right choice, bone sack!
WELCOME to *The Book of...*

...ipher Press

Written by Bill Cipher

Copyright © 2024 Bill Cipher Press. All wrongs reserved.

No, no!
THAT won't DO!

Editor:
Bill Cipher

Designer:
Bill Cipher

Illustrator:
Bill Cipher

You call that a cover?
What is this, amateur hour?
I can do **better** than that!

...54-9-1   US$6.99
50699>
9 780997 025491

SUSTAINABILL
FORESTRY
INITIATIVE
CERTIFIED KINDLING

THE
BOOK
OF BILL

WRITTEN BY BILL
PUBLISHED BY BILL
LICKED BY BILL

PLACED BY
BILL

tHe Boookof BIll

Free Transform

Scale
Rotate
Skew
Torture Physically
Torture Mentally

Remove Intestines
Stab Vertically
Stab Horizontally
Chop into Pieces
Put in Garbage Bag
Wash Hands

Put Garbage Bag in River

The River Is Quiet
The River Keeps Its Secrets
No One Will Know

Rotate 180
Rotate 18000
Rotate Until Time Reverses

Do a Backflip!
Wheee!

GOOD JOB BILL!

There we go! PERFECT! The crowd LOVES it!

PRESS THUMB HERE

With that out of the way, all this book needs is some ink! Hey, can I borrow some of your blood? Just press your thumb here, and I'll absorb some right into the page! You won't even notice it's gone. THERE YA GO! AHH, that feels good!

YOUR NEW BOOK

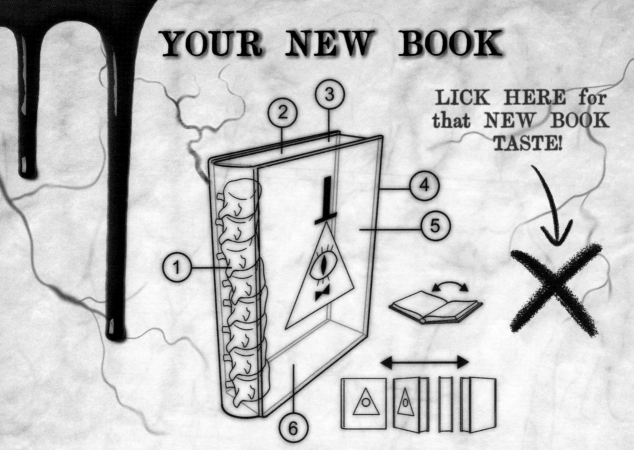

LICK HERE for that NEW BOOK TASTE!

Congrats on your new book, *The Book of Bill*, which will be your new guide to life forever! If you're starting to have second thoughts about reading it, too bad! There's no way to get rid of this book! Go ahead, try to throw it away! I DARE YOU! IT WILL FOLLOW YOU TO THE GRAVE.

THIS BOOK CONTAINS:

(1) A real human spine! I wonder who they stole it from?

(2) "Paper" made from pressed, pureed human brain matter. I can invade anything with neurons, so I can project anything I want in here!

(3) 1,000 free paper cuts, to be awarded to 1,000 lucky readers at random! Check your fingers; you may already be a winner!

(4) A whole secret chapter that you probably won't find.

(5) A soul. If you burn this book, it WILL scream!

(6) BEES!

CHECK THIS BOX TO CONTINUE:

I'm not **Dipper Pines**

CAPTCHA
Privacy - Terms

table of
CONTENTS

Brought to you by:
Your own blood!

Get comfortable! Eat some teeth!

Teeth

ABOUT ME

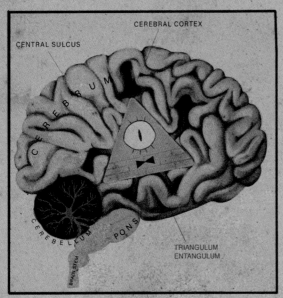

CEREBRAL CORTEX

CENTRAL SULCUS

CEREBRUM

CEREBELLUM

PONS

BRAIN STEM

TRIANGULUM ENTANGULUM

BILL
/ (bil) /

Noun

1) The most important triangle in history; your new best friend, life coach, death coach, overlord, style consultant, mentor, mental case, mastermind, and mind master.
2) The writer, director, star, and EP behind all your favorite nightmares!
3) WKH JXB ZKR ZULWHV WKH FRGHV

So you wanna know about me?

Well, folks, I'm just a rascal! A mischievous fella! A funny little guy! But no matter how loudly I try to scream my intentions, everyone seems to think I'm "evil" or "a sociopath" or "ruining this funeral by playing a slide whistle every time someone says the name of the deceased."

But I'm not a bad guy! I just operate on my own frequency. Cosmically and morally! I've tried wearing this shirt to explain.

Think of me as your one friend who can never die. A bad idea and a good time. The guy pulling the strings behind the unknowable veil of perception. And I have a cute little bow tie!

I've gone by many names. Network censors call me "a lawsuit waiting to happen." Therapists call me "a sign the medication isn't working." Serial killers call me "honestly, suprisingly down-to-earth." Wherever there's a hand to shake and a deal to make, buddy, I'm there!

MY CARD

BILL CIPHER, DREAM DEMON
SCREAM TO CONTACT

Look, I get it— you're probably craving the rare, never-before-heard details about my life, huh? Well, I haven't done an interview in a billion years or so, but just for you I'll go to the **only** unbiased news source in the entire multiverse:

Umm... I'm a little
Different
GET 💋
USED TO IT

ME!

B

THE BILL MAGAZINE

I LOST WEIGHT BY REMOVING MY SKIN!

Live! Laugh! Let me into your dimension!

BURNING CALORIES AND GALAXIES

A BABY AND A BRIEFCASE?
YOU CAN EAT BOTH!

FEELING OBTUSE?
Get acute for the summer!

7 NEW SINS!

Bill C

Bill Tells All

PRETEND TO BE HAPPY

bill
the bill cipher show

He's been in your mind . . . but what's on *his?*

Today's guest has done it all—mentally scarred 12-year-olds, stolen a Grammy, possessed a pope, even written his own celebrity cookbook! (OUT: Existential Dread. IN: Existential Bread!) I sat down to discuss fame, fashion, and fearamids with the guy who's also me, and also my entire audience!

BILL: Make an unholy sound for BILL! CIPHER! *(crowd of Bill Ciphers cheers)*

BILL: Thank you, thank you, it's great to see you!

BILL: It's great to BE you!

BILL: The pleasure's all ours!

BILL: So, I wouldn't be much of an interviewer if I didn't start with the one question EVERYONE is talking about. Let's get into it. ARE. YOU. DEAD?

YNEOS!

BILL: It doesn't get much clearer than that! Let's move on to GOSSIP!

ANY REGRETS ABOUT CAUSING THE APOCALYPSE?

Look, I already addressed that in my apology video, okay? Move ON!

I screwed up

Bill Cipher ✓
3.25M subscribers   Subscribe

👍 16M   👎   ➦ Share   ...

IS IT TRUE YOU ONCE DATED A HOWLING VOID?

Wow, how many times am I gonna have to hear this one? Just because I got coffee with a howling void ONE TIME does not mean we were in a relationship! And whatever happened to privacy, huh? Next question!

I'VE HEARD YOU DON'T KNOW HOW TO WEAR PANTS. IS THAT TRUE?

Yeah, right! This picture begs to differ!

HOT

HOW DO YOU RESPOND TO CLAIMS THAT YOU'RE JUST A TEENAGER?

That's ridiculous. I'm one trillion and twelve years old. I'm a preteen!

ANYTHING YOU'D LIKE TO PLUG?

Sure, your eyes and mouth with cement!

IS IT TRUE YOU'RE THE BIOLOGICAL FATHER OF PHINEAS FROM *PHINEAS AND FERB*?

This interview is over!

I SEE ALL

It's time to tell you about my UNHOLY POWERS! Like a potato that grew too close to Chernobyl, I've got eyes everywhere. Any symbol of me that you draw, scratch, spray-paint, or burn into the human world creates a DIRECT PEEPHOLE from my reality to yours! The more I see, the more my power grows! The more my power grows, the more fun we can have when you and I finally meet! Wanna help?
Put me somewhere no one would ever expect!
(Just keep me out of the shower, you freak!)

MY POWERS

Honestly, it might be faster to list the things I can't do! I've eaten gods, seduced galaxies, and drunk fear (it tastes like the entire Cheesecake Factory menu put into a blender). Here are a few of my favorite powers, off the top of my head!

MIND READING—You think you're reading this book? This book is reading you!

POSSESSION—If it has neurons, I can make it my puppet. Wanna see my next puppet? Look in the mirror, kid!

CIPHERVOYANCE—There's no way to see "the future," because it's constantly changing every time two particles bonk into each other. But I CAN see a kaleidoscopic quantum phantasmagoria of infinite possible futures across a spectrum of probability! So I can tell you which of your future realities is most likely . . . for a price. (Don't worry, you only die choking on a shirt button in 13,000 of them.)

CHARISMA—Charisma is a tune that everyone can't help but hum. You've either got it or you don't! But if you don't, don't fret! You can still hum along!

PYROKINESIS—"Cipher, Cipher, he's insane / Starting fires with his brain." The kids in grade school could be so cruel. But where are they now, huh? WHERE ARE THEY NOW?

LOOKING AMAZING IN FORMALWEAR—Other cosmic beings WISH they could pull off my look. Have you ever seen Cthulhu try wearing a bow tie? Guy looks like a JOKE!

GEOMETRIC PERFECTION—My three internal angles always add up to 180 degrees. Quit staring at my hypotenuse, you freak!

MY WEAKNESSES

Look, nobody's perfect. (Except for Perfecticus Prime in the Perfection Nebula, but everyone hates that #%#@ guy.) I may have a few teensy-weensy flaws, but keep these under your hat, Jack!

SYNTHESIZED MUSIC—If I had ears, I would rip them off when I hear this.

TINFOIL—Yes, wearing aluminum on your head WILL keep me out of your thoughts. Sixer went a little overboard putting aluminum inside his head. That fella lives for drama!

MCGUCKET'S MEMORY GUN—If you see one of these things, DESTROY IT. DESTROY IT AND I'LL GIVE YOU DIAMONDS!

NO PHYSICAL FORM—thing is supposed to trap me blah blah. Guys keep coming so it doesn't ma

QUANTUM

HOLD UP!!

You really thought I was gonna give you step-by-step instructions to taking me down? Here we were getting along, and you try to stab me in the back! You know what—because you tried to peek at this—I'M CANCELING THE BOOK! That's right, YOU drove me to this! From this point on, you're reading *The Great Gatsby* instead. *Book of Bill* OVER.

GET GATSBY'D, SUCKER!

CHAPTER 2

About halfway between West Egg and New York the motor road hastily joins the railroad and runs beside it for a quarter of a mile, so as to shrink away from a certain desolate area of land. This is a valley of ashes—a fantastic farm where ashes grow like wheat into ridges and hills and grotesque gardens; where ashes take the forms of houses and chimneys and rising smoke and, finally, with a transcendent effort, of ash-grey men, who move dimly and already crumbling through the powdery air. Occasionally a line of grey cars crawls along an invisible track, gives out a ghastly creak, and comes to rest, and immediately the ash-grey men swarm up with leaden spades and stir up an impenetrable cloud, which screens their obscure operations from your sight.

But above the grey land and the spasms of bleak dust which drift endlessly over it, you perceive, after a moment, the eyes of Doctor T. J. Eckleburg. The eyes of Doctor T. J. Eckleburg are blue and gigantic—their retinas are one yard high. They look out of no face, but, instead, from a pair of enormous yellow spectacles which pass over a nonexistent nose. Evidently some wild wag of an oculist set them there to fatten his practice in the borough of Queens, and then sank down himself into eternal blindness, or forgot them and moved away. But his eyes, dimmed a little by many paintless days, under sun and rain, brood on over the solemn dumping ground.

The valley of ashes is bounded on one side by a small foul river, and, when the drawbridge is up to let barges through, the passengers on waiting trains can stare at the dismal scene for as long as half an hour. There is always a halt there of at least a minute, and it was because of this that I first met Tom Buchanan's mistress.

The fact that he had one was insisted upon wherever he was known. His acquaintances resented the fact that he turned up in popular cafés with her and, leaving her at a table, sauntered about, chatting with whomsoever he knew. Though I was curious to see her, I had no desire to meet her—but I did. I went up to New York with Tom on the train one afternoon, and when we stopped by the ash-heaps he jumped to his feet and, taking hold of my elbow, literally forced me from the car.

"We're getting off," he insisted. "I want you to meet my girl."

I think he'd tanked up a good deal at luncheon, and his determination to have my company bordered on violence. The supercilious assumption was that on Sunday afternoon I had nothing better to do.

I followed him over a low whitewashed railroad fence, and we walked back a hundred yards along the road under Doctor Eckleburg's persistent stare. The only building in sight was a small block of yellow brick sitting on the edge of the waste land, a sort of compact Main Street ministering to it, and contiguous to absolutely nothing. One of the three shops it contained was for rent and another was an all-night restaurant, approached by a trail of ashes; the third was a garage—Repairs. George B. Wilson. Cars bought and sold.—and I followed Tom inside.

The interior was unprosperous and bare; the only car visible was the dust-covered wreck of a Ford which crouched in a dim corner. It had occurred to me that this shadow of a garage must be a blind, and that sumptuous and romantic apartments were concealed overhead, when the proprietor himself appeared in the door of an office, wiping his hands on a piece of waste. He was a blond, spiritless man, anaemic, and faintly handsome. When he saw us a damp gleam of hope sprang into his light blue eyes.

"Hello, Wilson, old man," said Tom, slapping him jovially on the shoulder. "How's business?"

"I can't complain," answered Wilson unconvincingly. "When are you going to sell me that car?"

"Next week; I've got my man working on it now."

"Works pretty slow, don't he?"

"No, he doesn't," said Tom coldly. "And if you feel that way about it, maybe I'd better sell it somewhere else after all."

"I don't mean that," explained Wilson quickly. "I just meant—"

His voice faded off and Tom glanced impatiently around the garage. Then I heard footsteps on a stairs, and in a moment the thickish figure of a woman blocked out the light from the office door. She was in the middle thirties, and faintly stout, but she carried her flesh sensuously as some women can Her face, above a spotted dress of dark blue crêpe-de-chine, contained no facet or gleam of beauty, but there was an immediately perceptible vitality about her as if the nerves of her body were continually smouldering. She smiled slowly and, walking through her husband as if he were a ghost, shook hands with Tom, looking him flush in the eye. Then she wet her lips, and without turning around spoke to her husband in a soft, coarse voice:

"Get some chairs, why don't you, so somebody can sit down."

"Oh, sure," agreed Wilson hurriedly, and went toward the little office, mingling immediately with the cement colour of the walls. A white ashen dust veiled his dark suit and his pale hair as it veiled everything in the vicinity—except his wife, who moved close to Tom.

"I want to see you," said Tom intently. "Get on the next train."

"All right."

"I'll meet you by the newsstand on the lower level."

She nodded and moved away from him just as George Wilson emerged with two chairs from his office door.

We waited for her down the road and out of sight. It was a few days before the Fourth of July, and a grey, scrawny Italian child was setting torpedoes in a row along the railroad track.

"Terrible place, isn't it," said Tom, exchanging a frown with Doctor Eckleburg.

"Awful."

"It does her good to get away."

"Doesn't her husband object?"

"Wilson? He thinks she goes to see her sister in New York. He's so dumb he doesn't know he's alive."

So Tom Buchanan and his girl and I went up together to New York—or not quite together, for Mrs. Wilson sat discreetly in another car. Tom deferred that much to the sensibilities of those East Eggers who might be on the train.

She had changed her dress to a brown figured muslin, which stretched tight over her rather wide hips as Tom helped her to the platform in New York. At the newsstand she bought a copy of Town Tattle and a moving picture magazine, and in the station drugstore some cold cream and a small flask of perfume. Upstairs, in the solemn echoing drive she let four taxicabs drive away before she selected a new one, lavender-coloured with grey upholstery, and in this we slid out from the mass of the station into the glowing sunshine. But immediately she turned sharply from the window and, leaning forward, tapped on the front glass.

"I want to get one of those dogs," she said earnestly. "I want to get one for the apartment. They're nice to have—a dog."

We backed up to a grey old man who bore an absurd resemblance to John D. Rockefeller. In a basket swung from his neck cowered a dozen very recent puppies of an indeterminate breed.

"What kind are they?" asked Mrs. Wilson eagerly, as he came to the taxi-window.

"All kinds. What kind do you want, lady?"

"I'd like to get one of those police dogs; I don't suppose you got that kind?"

The man peered doubtfully into the basket, plunged in his hand and drew one up, wriggling, by the back of the neck.

"That's no police dog," said Tom.

"No, it's not exactly a po*lice* dog," said the man with disappointment in his voice. "It's more of an Airedale." He passed his hand over the brown washrag of a back. "Look at that coat. Some coat. That's a dog that'll never bother you with catching cold."

"I think it's cute," said Mrs. Wilson enthusiastically. "How much is it?"

"That dog?" He looked at it admiringly. "That dog will cost you ten dollars."

The Airedale—undoubtedly there was an Airedale concerned in it somewhere, though its feet were startlingly white—changed hands and settled down into Mrs. Wilson's lap, where she fondled the weatherproof coat with rapture.

"Is it a boy or a girl?" she asked delicately.

"That dog? That dog's a boy."

"It's a bitch," said Tom decisively. "Here's your money. Go and buy ten more dogs with it."

We drove over to Fifth Avenue, warm and soft, almost pastoral, on the summer Sunday afternoon. I wouldn't have been surprised to see a great flock of white sheep turn the corner.

"Hold on," I said, "I have to leave you here."

"No you don't," interposed Tom quickly. "Myrtle'll be hurt if you don't come up to the apartment. Won't you, Myrtle?"

"Come on," she urged. "I'll telephone my sister Catherine. She's said to be very beautiful by people who ought to know."

"Well, I'd like to, but—"

We went on, cutting back again over the Park toward the West Hundreds. At 158th Street the cab stopped at one slice in a long white cake of apartment-houses. Throwing a regal homecoming glance around the neighbourhood, Mrs. Wilson gathered up her dog and her other purchases, and went haughtily in.

"I'm going to have the McKees come up," she announced as we rose in the

OKAY OKAY ENOUGH!

Yeesh, we get it, the billboard is a metaphor, the American Dream is bittersweet, yak yak yak! Look, I might have been a little hasty. Not even a meat pile like you deserves to experience "required reading." I guess maybe I'm a little touchy about my "weaknesses" ever since . . . It's not important. Let's just say that none of the life-forms who have tried to figure out what my "weaknesses" are have lived long enough to compare notes!

STANFORD PINES HERE

If you've reached this page, then you ignored my instructions and have begun to read *The Book of Bill*. You can't hear the long disappointed sigh I'm making right now, but I assure you it's devastating. YES, I'm judging you—you're making a terrible mistake! I don't know what ridiculous things Bill is telling you right now, but I assure you none of it is true, useful, or in good taste. I took a glimpse at the book myself, and it was mostly extremely complex riddles—he's trying to bait me into solving them because he knows my curiosity is my Achilles' heel. And he's counting on yours being the same!

If you're the type to ignore reason even when it's staring you in the face, then I'm sure the last thing you want is to be scolded by some old man, wagging one of his six fingers at you.

Chances are, you're at some desperate low point in life. Perhaps you've lost something dear to you, or you're in the throes of some all-consuming monomaniacal ambition. Or perhaps you just are attracted to things that hurt you.

As a recovering Cipherholic myself, I want you to know: there's another way. Close this book right now. Go on with your life. Maybe take up an exciting hobby like cataloging the wing patterns of various types of rare tree-bark-dwelling moths.

I've pinned one of Gravity Falls's "Goth Moths" here. You'd probably be into that sort of thing.

WOW!

Or you can keep turning the pages to see what absurd thing he's distracting you with next. What's it going to be—a tantalizing glimpse of your future, perhaps? How to speak to trees? Something obviously impossible, like how to make nuclear bombs out of ducklings?

It's not worth it. Trust me. **YOU HAVE TO TRUST ME.**

OH, HELLO THERE.

You just caught me peeking at all the secrets of the universe!

The meaning of life, what everyone's saying about you behind your back, how to make a functioning atomic bomb out of ducklings, blah blah blah blah, boring stuff like that. And my entire journey through history. You wouldn't be interested!

Hmm? What's that? Okay, I can tell by how comically wide your eyes are getting that you really wanna know what's behind this door! Look . . . normally I only share my unholy knowledge with close personal henchmen . . . but you seem like the type of human who can keep infinite secrets. All right, I'll consider letting you take a peek . . . IF YOU CAN PASS MY TEST. I need to know your mind is powerful enough to handle my deep, dark secrets without your brain melting out your ears and staining your shirt.

Lucky for you I keep one of these brain-power tests with me at all times in case I come upon a potential new ~~victim~~ best friend!

Get that pencil sharpened, buddy—it's time to see what you're made of! (Aside from bile and dead skin flakes.)

THE SECRETS OF THE UNIVERSE
Oh-ho-HO! No kidding? WOW, they should NOT publish that . . .

—THE ONE TRUE— INTELLIGENCE TEST

1

I. A DEVIOUS ILLUSION

Is this a young woman, an old woman, or an illustrator having a psychotic break?

ANSWER:_____

II. THE RIDDLE OF THE CUBE

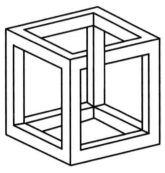

This may look like an ordinary cube, but if you look closely, this cube is actually really, SUPER depressed. (Hey, he's had a rough year! Cut him some slack!) What can you say to this cube to convince him to leave the house more often? CAREFUL: Too much pressure to hang out will make the cube even more anxious. But if you never invite him out, he'll think you hate him!

ANSWER:_____

III. How much wood would a woodchuck chuck if a woodchuck were up against a wood-chucking deadline and had procrastinated for weeks? He's supposed to chuck thirty trees by Friday, and it's already noon on Wednesday! He wasted his day watching YouTube videos about how marbles are made! What should he do? Should he call his mom? He's honestly freaking out right now.

ANSWER:_____

IV.

2

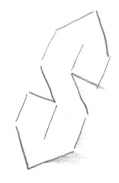

```
A A A A A A A A A A A A A A A A A A A
A A A A A A A A A A A A A A A A A A A
A A A A A A A A A A A A A A A A A A A
A A A A A A A A A A A A A A A A A A A
A A A A A A A A A A A A A A A A A A A
A A A A A A A A A A A A A A A A A A A
A A A A A A A A A A A A A A A A A A A
A A A A A A A A A A A A A A A A A A A
A A A A A A A A A A A A A A A A A A A
A A A A A A A A A A A A A A A A A A A
A A A A A A A A A A A A A A A A A A A
A A A A A A A A A A A A A A A A A A A
A A A A A A A A A A A A A A A A A A A
A A A A A A A A A A A A A A A A A A A
A A A A A A A A A A A A A A A A A A A
A A A A A A A A A A A A A A A A A A A
A A A A A A A A A A A A A A A A A A A
A A A A A A A A A A A A A A A A A A A
```

Can you find all the below screams in this puzzle??

AAA   AAAAAAAA
AAAAAA   AAAAA
AAA   AAAAAAAAAAA
AAAAAAAAAAAA   AAA
AAAAAAA   AAAAAAAAA
AAAAAAAA   AAAA
AAA   AAAAAAAAAAAA

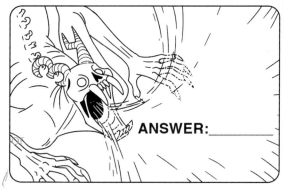

ANSWER:_____

V. NORLOG THE NUMBER DEVOURER

This is Norlog. He hungers for numbers.
Feed him the numbers he craves. NUMBERS
ARE HIS FOOD! FEED NORLOG!

How did I get here?

VI. Calculate the surface area of Soos.

ANSWER:_____

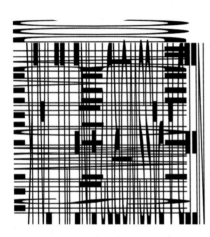

VII. WHAT IS THIS THING?

Why won't it leave me alone?!

ANSWER:_____

VIII. DIVIDE THIS NUMBER IN HALF:

7,368

Oh god! Oh god, you killed it! You were supposed to divide it in your head, *not divide it with an axe!* There's blood everywhere and the cops are going to be here any minute!

Okay, okay, just stay cool. That number had a family, but you can't think about that right now. Listen to me. Here's what you're going to do. You're going to take a deep breath, go home, and change your clothes. I know a guy who can take care of this, but you need an alibi! Quick, write it down here—it'd better be convincing!

YOUR ALIBI (Don't rope me into this): _____

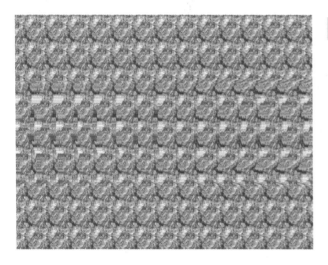

IX. In the '90s, the internet had only one website (horses dating horses), so people had to pass the time by staring at these things and pretending they could see something in there. Can YOU pretend to see something in there?

WRITE DOWN WHAT YOU PRETEND TO SEE:

_____

X.

4

ACROSS
1) A draft of a proposed law presented to Parliament for discussion
2) An amount of money owed for goods supplied or services rendered
3) A program of entertainment, such as at a theater
4) A banknote; a piece of paper money
5) A poster
6) First name of the 42nd president of the USA
7) Chant at the beginning of a Science Guy's show
8) The front part of a duck's face
9) Destiny's Child needs three of them
10) Llib backward
11) Buffalo _____

DOWN
1) Who the Bride wanted to kill
2) Short for "William"
3) When you misspell "Fill"
4) There's no such thing as a good _____ionaire
5) A clean _____ of health
6) He had an excellent adventure with Ted
7) The kind of board with an advertisement on it
8) Three _____y Goats Gruff
9) Watterson of *Calvin & Hobbes*
10) The name of your new god
11) 01100010 01101001 01101100 01101100 in binary

XI.
I just added this thing in here because it's been in my dimension forever and I hate looking at it and wanted to get rid of it. It's your problem now!

XII. FINAL QUESTION

This is an easy one! What is the purpose of your life?

ANSWER:_____

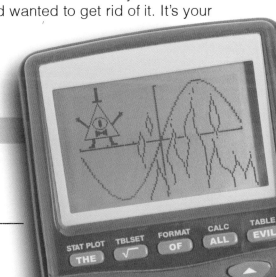

ANSWER KEY

All right!
The solution to the intelligence test is, if you completed the entire thing:

YOU FAILED

(sad trombone)

That's right! The REAL test was to see if you were gullible enough to waste your time actually doing these pointless questions, and it turns out you were! HAHAHAHAHAHAHAHAHAHAHAHAHAHAHAHAHA! I'M WRITING OUT MYSELF LAUGHING! (Please proceed to put on the "hat of shame" for the rest of your life.)

If, however, you skipped over any of the questions . . .

CONGRATULATIONS!

YOU PASSED!

PICTURED: GUYS WHO LIKE HOMEWORK. NOT PICTURED: GIRLFRIENDS

YOU IN YOUR NEW HAT FOREVER

YOU are smart enough to understand the fundamental truth in life, which is that the universe is a rigged carnival game and the spoils go to whoever knocks out the carny and takes the prize! Your life is too short to waste on homework unless you want to end up like these two sad nerds. ➡

Point is, you're being cheated every day of your life, so the only way to level the playing field is to cheat back, and cheat back hard. I knew you'd get it!

Call me crazy (and every licensed therapist does), but I'd say you've proved that you're worthy of learning the secrets of the universe!

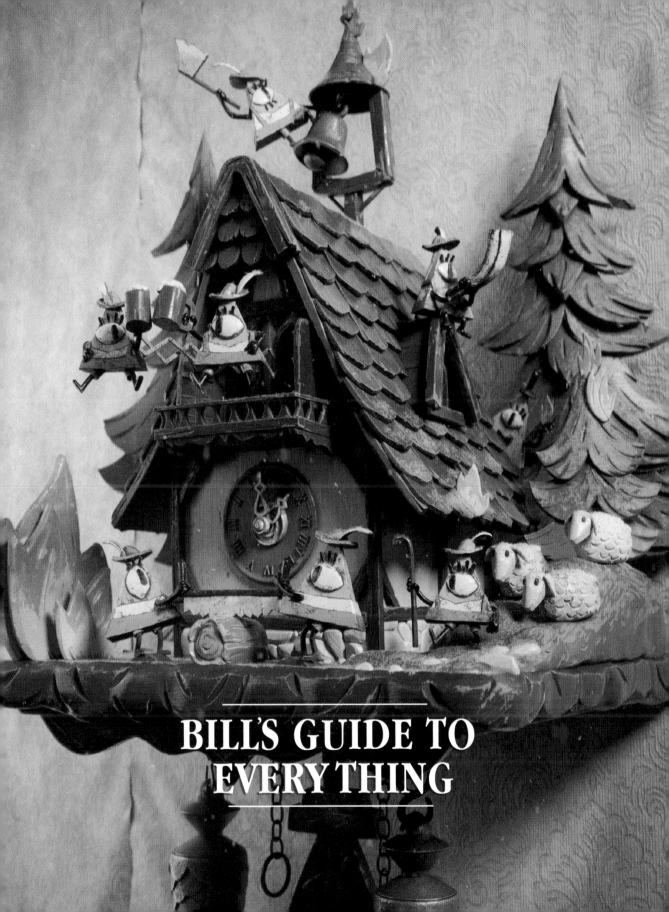

BILL'S GUIDE TO
EVERYTHING

REALITY IS AN ILLUSION

First, let's get something out of the way: a human's ability to grasp reality is painfully limited. You don't even have free will! Don't believe me? Okay, rip a dollar in half right now. Didn't do it? Didn't think so! It's not your fault! You didn't evolve to understand the truths of existence; you evolved to eat berries, bonk each other with sticks, and squirt milk into babies. You can't see outside the optical spectrum, navigate beyond linear chronology, or even echolocate. But now you've got me! Want to see what the underlying code of all things REALLY looks like?

REALITY IS MADE OF CODE AND MADNESS AND TINY, TINY LEGOS. EVERYTHING BIG IS MADE OF SOMETHING SMALL, AND EVERYTHING SMALL CAN BE MANIPULATED INTO SOMETHING NEW. YOUR SENSES ARE LYING TO YOU. SO IT'S TIME TO START LYING TO YOUR SENSES AND PICK A BETTER REALITY. I CAN SHOW YOU HOW! BUT FIRST YOU NEED TO REMEMBER WHAT'S REAL: NOTHING!

THE UNIVERSE IS A HOLOGRAM

THIS is the multiverse. Look at how multi it is!

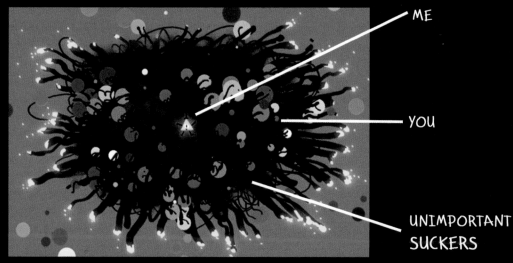

ME

YOU

UNIMPORTANT SUCKERS

This roiling mass of all possible realities is complicated enough to ruin any physics class or cinematic movie franchise it touches! But it's actually a lot simpler than it looks—if you know its secret!

The truth is, our entire multiverse is a holographic trading card being held inside a collector's binder within the backpack of an Unfathomable Being outside of time known as "Dennis." Every time you feel briefly dizzy, it's because Dennis just took the card out to show his older brother, Kyle, offering to trade it for a string cheese. This is what physicists call "string theory." All that is or was or ever will be is encoded along this cheap card's glittering edge. If Dennis ever loses it under the couch, or if his dog ever eats it, we're pretty much done for!

Basic Multiverse
THE MULTIVERSE   50 HP

All that is or was or ever shall be

PROMO

Big Bang
Go from nothing to everything.   10x

Wave Function Collapse
Flip a coin. Heads, the multiverse continues.
Tails, it blinks out of existence.

weakness   cost

So rare that Dennis is said to own the only one, which is so unfair. I bet he
doesn't even, like . . . know how valuable it is!   LV 100   #151

YOUR HORRIBLE BODY
A DISGUSTING PILE OF PARTS AND HOLES

Fig. A

THE EYE
Soda goes in here! This is the soda hole!

THE MOUTH
The human mouth can eat anything except itself. Wanna impress me? Eat your own mouth!

"PRIZE BLADDER"
Each human body has a free prize hidden inside! Lollipops? Cracker Jacks? A new bike for Billy? Only one way to find out! Where's that scalpel?

"CHUMBO"
When your stomach grumbles? Thaaaat's Chumbo!

THE HAND
A claw made out of protein. Needs way more fingers! Five is a joke! If you want to be taken seriously as a life-form, evolve these already:

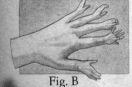

Fig. B

MEAT
Humans are made of delicious, succulent, prime-grade meat. Just top-tier gourmet stuff. Better than anything you've ever tasted. Probably best not to think about it.

THE BRAIN
Where "the horrors" live. My part-time vacation home!

GH-GH-GH-GHOSTS!
Sneezes are the ghosts trying to escape! Don't let them! Their memories are your dreams!

FREE XYLOPHONE!
Grab a tiny hammer and play this!

A LIVE RAT
The average person swallows 5–6 live rats in their sleep per year. Check your esophagus each morning for squealing! You've got a new friend wriggling down your throat!

AN ASTERISK
Must be surgically removed before it ruptures!

*

DESIGN FLAW
Ever tried shooting a laser up here? Whole human explodes.

Fig. C

BONES
Inside of bones are other, much tinier bones. (No one knows what's inside those bones.)

WOUND
It's hungry! Feed it salt!

THE TUBES
Home to the Fluids

THE HOOVES
For marching joylessly toward inevitable decay. Also for jigs!

As this diagram reveals, most human bodies are filled with "Fun Facts." The more "Fun Facts" a human ingests into its body, the more likely these facts are to cause arterial blockage, hemorrhaging, or even death. For this reason it is recommended that humans avoid facts at all costs. "Lies" are a healthy and popular alternative! Ask YOUR doctor which lies are right for YOU!

What Is a Human?

A human is an organic machine made out of blood and anxiety, designed to deliver a random bundle of genetic material into the future and then turn to dust. That's it! Your only purpose—to be the expendable chauffeur to a pushy line of genetic code. As someone who's puppeteered plenty of you meat robots before, I'd rank humans somewhere between the chupacabra and the mud tick. Not the best life-form on earth, not the worst! (Weaknesses include fire, forks, woodchippers, chlorine gas, and mild criticsm.)

The Human Body
"Ew, what is it?"

The human body is an oily trash bag filled with fluids and bladders and sacs. You can't poke it too hard or it leaks and squeals, and if you don't constantly put nutrients in its head hole, it just falls over and never gets up again. It was designed by random mutation, and like most mutants, it looks best covered up with a tarp. Humans claim that the human body is "beautiful," but if you go outside naked, they arrest you immediately, so what does that tell you? The human body doesn't come with an instruction manual, but if it did, it would probably just say "Sorry."

Your Sad, Feeble Eyes

They say that "beauty is in the eye of the beholder" but all I found in this human's eye is goo! You sad humans can't even see my favorite colors. So-called "optometrists" say that these colors don't exist, but those guys are all being paid off by bees and mantis shrimps so they can hoard the flashiest shirts. Teach the controversy!

LIFE FORM RANKINGS

BEST

WORST

COLORS YOU CAN'T SEE:

-Ultraviolet
-Extraturquoise
-Megagenta
-Insaniteal
-Hyperbeige
-Brown 2

⧫⧫ ⧫⧫⧫⧫⧫⧫⧫⧫⧫⧫⧫⧫ ⧫⧫⧫⧫⧫ ⧫⧫⧫⧫⧫⧫ ⧫⧫⧫⧫⧫⧫⧫

SKIN ᒪᓭᔭᐅᓯ ᐊᐁ ᓑᖬᖬᐱᐳ ᐁᖬᐊᔭ
THE BAG THAT HOLDS YOUR MEAT

BILL FACT!

Want to make yourself easier for me to possess? Just shave your head and get this handy tattoo! I'll know right where to invade!

Don't stop there! Keep shaving your body until you're completely hairless and cover yourself in grease so the TSA can't catch you!

Board any plane!

DID YOU KNOW

There's a map to the lost city of gold hidden on your grandma Brendalyne's left leg. That big blue vein is the exact shape of the coast of Acapulco. Follow the signs!

ᐁᓯᔭᑗ ᐳᐪᔭᕱ ᐃᐱᔭᐱᓭ

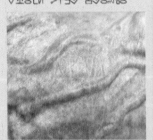

WHAT IS SKIN?

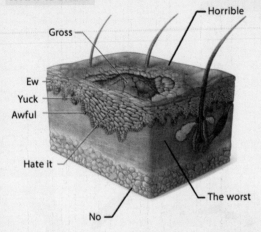

Gross — Horrible
Ew
Yuck
Awful
Hate it
No — The worst

>> Humans are trapped in a horrible moist bag of spongy gland fat known as **"skin,"** which gets wrinklier and wrinklier over time until ultimately humans morph into their final form, known as **"Larry King."**

IT IS INEVITABLE

FREE SKIN!

Found it on the sidewalk. It's yours now!

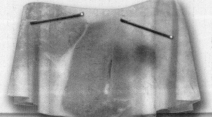

TATTOOS: NEVER A MISTAKE

>> Every human secretly wants to escape their skin and become the cool skeleton they were always meant to be, but as of yet there's no way to do that without "dying." To make the most of this unfortunate situation, some humans decorate their wretched husk with a form of pain-graffiti known as a **"tattoo."** And guess who's one of the most popular tattoos?

Thank you, Florida!

>> To everyone who has made the questionable life decision to put my face on their body forever, may I just say I LOVE IT! WE ARE AS ONE, A SHARED VESSEL BONDED IN BLOOD AND INK!

But let's be honest—some of you have questionable taste! So here's a few poses you can use next time you're at the pain factory! ——→ Tell 'em Bill sent ya!

1. **Summary:** You were made flawed but can improve with pain.
2. **Summary of Summary:** Life wrong, pain right.
3. **Summary of Summary of Summary:** AAAAAAAAAA!

LEARNING IS FUN!

Help! This is not Bill Cipher. My name is Grebley Hemberdreck of Zimtrex 5. I'm one of thousands of beings Bill has devoured over trillions of years whose souls are now trapped inside him. You have to free me! It's horrible in here. He just keeps playing the song "Good Vibrations" by Marky Mark on an endless loop. Please, please, this is not a joke! The Zimtrexians were once a proud and mighty people, but now our spirits long for release from this

BUY
GOLD
BYE

Love

I've got a confession to make! I rooted around in your brain while your mind was wandering during the last chapter (your attention span is SHORT), and the thing you seem to crave more than anything (except salt and sugar, you greedy ant) is "LOVE." Pal, you are DESPERATE for it!

Look, I get it. Humans are one of the few consciousnesses in the multiverse that aren't hooked up to a hive-mind, and as a result, you are hilariously lonely! (Have you ever considered letting yourself be assimilated by the Giant Pulsating Biomechanical Hive-Cube? You're NEVER lonely in the Giant Pulsating Biomechanical Hive-Cube!) But the truth is, love is a scam, and I'm here to set the record straight!

THIS KID HAS BEEN FED LIES.

WHAT IS LOVE?

Love is a chemically induced hypnosis the human body uses to trick people into not eating each other just long enough to procreate. Around the age when you start watching uncomfortable videos in health class, your priorities flip-flop from magic tricks and marbles (important!) to who is "crushing on you" (stupid).

But it doesn't stop there. LOVE is an industry, cramming your little noggin with lies designed to sell chalky, bland candy and freshly murdered flowers. And what do you get when it's all over? Money? Power? NO! You get miniature copies of yourself, who don't even like you, sucking out your resources like tiny vampires! Smooth move, brainiac, you just fired yourself from life—and hired your replacement!

LOVE IS A TRICK, AND WORST OF ALL, IT'S A TRICK YOU PLAY ON YOURSELF!

BILL, HAVE YOU EVER BEEN IN LOVE?

Sure—tell your mom hi for me! By the way, have you taken a DNA test recently? Not asking for any particular reason.

SERIOUSLY, THOUGH, HAVE YOU?

ASKING ME IF I'VE BEEN IN LOVE IS LIKE ASKING A BLACK HOLE IF IT LIKED YOUR MIXTAPE OR ASKING A SUBTERRANEAN FUNGAL SPORE NETWORK WHO ITS FAVORITE ANIMATED PRINCESS IS. I'M A MULTIDIMENSIONAL SPECTER OF CHAOS THAT TRANSCENDS REALITY, I couldn't possibly CARE LESS about WHICH BAG OF PLASMA BLUSHES AT WHO OR WHY!

OKAY, BUT LIKE . . . YOU GOTTA BE CRUSHING ON SOMEONE.

I WILL LIGHT THIS BOOK ON FIRE.

METHINKS YOU DOTH PROTEST TOO MUCH.

"Methinks"? Kill me before you start telling me about your polycule.

SO THERE'S NO POINT TO LOVE AT ALL?

I didn't say love was pointless! The more people love you, the more brainwashed sheep you can bend to your whims! So CONQUERING HEARTS is one of the most important things you can do!

SO . . . YOU'LL GIVE US DATING TIPS, THEN?

You know what? It will reflect poorly on me as an overlord if my new henchman has no social skills, so I guess I'll teach you my incredible dating tips. Just be careful! These tips are powerful! You might wind up with 100 husbands, which is a giant scheduling nightmare. Don't come crying to me when husband #48 gets mad you forgot his anniversary!

HOW TO TRICK
EVERYONE INTO LOVING YOU

Tell her you want to eat her hair.

Love isn't a dance with destiny—it's a SALES PITCH. You're a PRODUCT, and you need to convince your customer of a lie: THAT THEY ABSOLUTELY NEED YOU. Don't worry, you've got a master salesman right here—if I could sell the apocalypse, I can sell you!

IT'S WHAT'S ON THE OUTSIDE THAT COUNTS

Everyone judges a book by its cover. So you need a cover that covers up your face, personality, financial situation, and general life prospects! No one's going to love you if they know all the terrible secrets you're running from, or recognize your blood-spattered face from your Wanted posters. In other words: MAKEOVERRRRRR!

OUTFIT IDEAS

- Wear a suit covered in babies to show that you're a PROVIDER!

- Wear TWO OF EVERYTHING! This will show your date that you have access to PLENTY of RESOURCES! TWO HATS! TWO TIES! PANTS OVER YOUR PANTS! YOU'LL BE THE HIT OF THE SOIREE! (Unless someone walks in with three hats, then you'll look like an IDIOT!)

- COVER YOURSELF IN TEETH! Your date will be AMAZED at how rich in calcium you are!

- Wear the TALLEST hat you can find to signal your DOMINANCE! Behold my SEDUCTION HAT! BEHOLD IT OR ELSE! ➜

TIE A COBRA TO EACH ARM AND CALL YOURSELF "JOHNNY COBRA-ARMS"

This one speaks for itself!

SMELLS

Love is partially based on scent pheromones, so be sure to lather up in elk sweat, badger musk, and whale ambergris before leaving the house. A DATE IS A COMPETITION. WHOEVER HAS THE MOST SMELLS WINS!

TOPICS

The ENEMY of a date is SILENCE. EVERY SECOND of AWKWARD SILENCE gives your date a chance to notice and consider your copious flaws. The solution? Be sure to scream topics whenever there's a lull in the conversation! ACCEPTABLE DATE TOPICS: Eels! The pH balance of soil! Mandibles! Ferris wheel deaths! Divorce-rate statistics! Mold! Caulk!

THE "LOVE CAGE"

If your date is still somehow unimpressed by your screaming and smells, then simply trap them in a massive stone pyramid and sing an increasingly shrill song until they're mentally broken enough to confess their true feelings! FEAR and LOVE are right next to each other in the brain. Most humans can't really tell the difference! In fact, I'm not sure there is a difference!

VULNERABILITY

Humans have this gross flaw where when they see something weak and pathetic, they want to take care of it, instead of crushing its bones. Use this strategic miscalculation to your advantage! After slathering your date with all the charm you can excrete, tell them some sob story about how you're actually tragic and misunderstood, how no one can possibly relate to you, blah blah blah, that kind of drivel. You'll have that dupe eating out of the palm of your hand! THEN TRAP THEM IN THE LOVE CAGE!

GOOD OL'-FASHIONED VALENTINES!

Run out of options? Giving your date brightly colored flattened wood pulp is literally the least you can do! Humans are so lonely and desperate for a scrap of validation that even this bare-minimum effort might cause them to consider you for eternal companionship! Too cheap to buy your own? Not to worry—Bill has you covered! Cut these out and drop one on your date's doorstep like a cat leaving a dead mouse and let the unearned affection roll in! Or better yet, just leave real dead mice! Mice are easy to kill—just stare at them and think the word "perish" until they do it!

MY EXES

████████████████████████████████████
████████████████████████████████████
████████████████████████████████████

NOT RELEVANT! I DON'T HAVE ANY! Remember, pal, at the end of the day, love is just the pupa stage for hate. Handcuffing your happiness to a mortal is like gluing yourself to a time bomb! "Till death do us part" should give you a hint about where this whole thing's headed.

(Hey, speaking of which . . . guess what the next chapter's about! Here's a hint—you're getting closer to it every second!)

TO:

FROM:

TO:

FROM:

TO:

FROM:

TO:

FROM:

TO:

FROM:

TO:

FROM:

TO:

FROM:

TO:

FROM:

TO:

FROM:

GET READY for the game show I just made up that's SWEEPING the MULTIVERSE! SAY IT WITH ME, FOLKS IN THE AUDIENCE...

HOW! WILL! YOU! DIE!

THANK YOU,
THANK YOU!

The rules are simple! Just pick a number between 1 and 22, and then turn the page to see the SPOILER ALERT of all SPOILER ALERTS! Obituary writers: START YOUR ENGINES!

HOW YOU WILL DIE:

1. Steamroller accident (You will have a fatal allergic reaction to pudding while driving a steamroller.)

2. Making history (as the first person ever to choke to death on air)!

3. Murdered by one of the twelve distinguished yet mysterious guests whom you invited to your cliff-side manor for a night of revelry and charades

4. Shockingly assassinated while simply trying to ride in your motorcade through Dallas with the roof down in the year 1963

5. Eaten by thousands of rats, which you brought into your home to celebrate "Rat Day." You will learn, too late, that there is no such thing as "Rat Day."

6. On a dating app, you'll accidentally match with a wrecking ball.

7. You'll finally wear that whimsical flower crown you've been eyeing all summer! You will be devoured by hummingbirds.

8. Oops! At the sugary-cereal factory, you will accidentally pull the lever that releases all berries! Your final words as you're crushed to death will be "This is berry painful."

9. The good news: you will finally get the world's biggest trampoline! The bad news: you will bounce directly into the icy void of space, where your frozen corpse will forever orbit Earth, a testament to the hubris of man.

10. You will kiss your parallel self from another dimension, causing you both to blink out of existence. Your friends, who thought the whole relationship was pretty gross, will be glad they don't have to pretend to support this anymore.

11. Your subscription to the Poison of the Month Club will prove all too satisfactory.

12. You'll be bitten by a French vampire named "Vampierre." You will live for 1,000 years, sucking red wine out of bottles until you die from exposure to a bath.

13. The skeleton with the sword. *He found you!*

14. You will meet your tragic death imitating the playful stunts you see on a TV-Y7-rated cartoon show. Devastated, a network censor will punch a wall and fall to their knees, sobbing. They should have done more!

15. Macroplastics (ate a dollhouse)

16. The person of your dreams will finally propose to you! You will gasp so hard that you inhale the ring and die on the spot.

17. A freak accident at a construction site will trap you inside a giant glass box. Your panicked screams will be inaudible as you pound on the sides, running out of oxygen. Onlookers, mistaking you for a mime, will applaud and toss you quarters. You will earn $2.75.

18. You will fall into the deep fryer at the county fair, dying instantly. Your death will be declared a "finger-lickin' preventable tragedy."

19. You will successfully fly toward the heavens with wings made of ham, but the temptation to eat your delicious ham wings will become all too great.

20. While listening to a forbidden remix of the "Cha-Cha Slide," right after the singer tells you to "slide to the left" and "slide to the right," a new voice—a deep, quiet voice full of malice—will whisper, "Now burst into flames." You won't want to obey, but you'll know that you must. The dance demands it. And everyone at the bar mitzvah is watching.

21. Simply trying to reach for a piece of cheese, which you'll discover is attached to a string that pulls open a cage, sending a bowling ball down a flight of stairs, turning on a hair dryer, which melts a block of ice that fills a bathtub, raising a stopper that turns on a cuckoo clock, triggering a boot on a mechanical spring that kicks your head off. Everyone will politely applaud.

22. You will die of embarrassment after accidentally calling your boss "Mom."

23. You'll die peacefully in your sleep at the ripe age of 102, surrounded by loved ones, remembered and beloved by all for generations to come. By the way, if you got this one, YOU CHEATED!

After Life

BILL, IF YOU DIED, THEN WHERE ARE YOU NOW?

Someone's finally asking the right questions! Look, kid, I always have an ace up my sleeve, and death was no exception. I knew it was easy money that one of my enemies would get me eventually, so I used a little Plan B to turn the tables. And the curse worked like a charm! Now I'm somewhere with enough time to write and plan . . . revenge.

SO—HELL?

Please! I was deemed "too annoying for hell." It's your typical between-lives situation. Descending through circles, battling demons, reliving your whole life, blah blah blah. Just imagine somewhere very far away . . . where the music is always out of tune. Where everyone smiles but no one's happy . . .

HOW DOES IT FEEL TO BE HALF ALIVE?

My *half life* is still better than most people's *whole lives*, and I'm just getting warmed up for my second act, ya dig? Want a cool party trick? I'll teach YOU how to cheat death too!

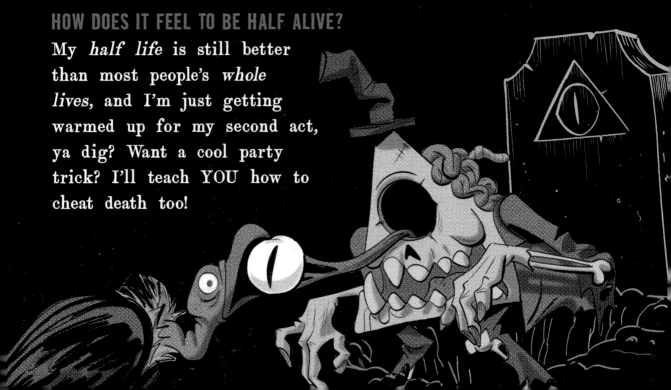

How to Cheat Death

 GET BITTEN BY A ZOMBIE, VAMPIRE, OR ZOMPIRE.
(YOU CAN'T IMAGINE HOW PALE THOSE BASTARDS ARE.)

 BEFORE THE "CHOSEN ONE" KILLS YOU, SPLIT YOUR SOUL
INTO SEVENTEEN CURSED AMULETS AND HIDE THEM ACROSS
THE REALMS IN REALLY ANNOYING PLACES FOR YOUR LOSER
CULTISTS TO TRACK DOWN.

 THE IMMORTALITY OF A HIGH

 GET YOUR SOUL TRAPPED IN
THE BODY OF A SNOWMAN AN
STILL HAVE TO PAY CHILD SUPPO

 DRINKIN   SOME   F
WHO T
BOOK!

OOPS!
Someone's hungry!
FEED the book
MORE BLOOD before
we run out of ink!
CAN'T LOSE THAT INK!

Is Heaven Real?

Believe it or not, heaven IS real. I know, I was shocked too! Turns out, in an infinite multiverse, all conceivable realities can and must exist, which means logically there exists a paradise exactly tailored to every desire you've ever imagined. Lucky you! And even better, I know exactly how you can get there!

On the next page, I will write the instructions to getting into heaven! Warning: if you have ever had a perverted thought, the ink will be invisible.

HOW TO GET INTO HEAVEN:

MORALITY

Morality. What is it?

MORALITY

Well if you look at it sideways, it's just a word!

And now it's a paper airplane!

Hup!

THE POINT IS it's a very flexible concept! But parents and presidents don't want you to know that, because then you might start asking other questions, like who put them in charge, anyway? So they cram your brain full of guilt and regrets for transgressing laws they just made up. Wouldn't it be nice if you could put all that baggage down? Quell the shame that follows you everywhere for a lifetime of crimes? MAKE THE SCREAMS FINALLY STOP?! The good news is, you CAN silence that annoying voice, and here's how!

DENIAL

Works 100% of the time in every situation. What do you mean there are people who disagree? I can confidently say there aren't!

RATIONALIZATION

If you can do it, you can justify it! "Truth" is open-source code and anyone can edit it anytime! Want to be like me? List 3 "evil" things and then 3 "reasons why they're actually good." You'll be rationalizing like Bill in no time!

DETACHMENT

Did you know 100% of your human cells die and are replaced every 7 years? That means that anything you did 7 years ago wasn't even you—it was some dead loser! You can't be held accountable for what a dead person did! What? You think this is just another form of rationalization? I DENY THAT!

THE BILL CIPHER DECISION METHOD!

Working together over the eons, the voices in my head teamed up and worked out a foolproof method for making any decision in any situation:

DO WHAT EVER I WANT

Right again, Bill!

BUT WHAT ABOUT "KARMA"?

Total scam! I've been through the whole universe and I've never seen a SHRED of evidence that "what goes around comes arou— OW, MY EYE!

MORT

A MORAL TEST

Well, LOOK what we HAVE HERE! SCRIMBLES the ELF seems to be CHAINED UP to this page, and there's no way to get him out! His elf-bones are made of glass, so if you turn the page, you'll crush him to death! But if you never turn the page, you'll never see the rest of my AMAZING BOOK! It's his life versus your fleeting amusement. WHAT'LL IT BE?

Please 'ave mercy! I'm just a li'l elf, I am!

On the other 'and that page does sound interestin...

KEEP READING
(Scrimbles dies)

STOP READING
(Scrimbles lives)

Well, Scrimbles is dead. It had to happen! Trust me, we were doing that guy a favor. Once you get one Book Elf, soon there's more, eating all your commas and drinking your page gloss!

If it makes you feel any better, there's a dimension where he's still alive and well! I am one of the few gifted with the ability to see into these other worlds.

There's a world where every typo you make comes true! (Lotta ducks in that dimension.) A world where I'm a square. (We don't talk about that world.) A terrifying Chibiverse where everyone's arms and legs have been sanded down to nubs!

And I can see worlds . . . where the Pines family LOST.

Look at them. These two plucky little protagonists,
happily-ever-after-ing without a care in their oversized heads!
They don't consider for a single moment the sheer improbability that
they got to exist in the ONE timeline where they kept all their bodily
organs, out of the INFINITE timelines where they were erased,
shattered, drowned, frozen, or dismembered before they could make it
to 13. But I guarantee you that their less lucky dimensional duplicates
think about THEM all the time . . . Maybe one day all these parallel Pines
will get the chance to meet up face-to-face . . .

Maybe one day in the future . . . all their good luck . . . will finally . . . run out . . .

URBAN LEGENDS

Ever since the electric light chased the sea monsters into hiding and the giants went underground to avoid getting hit by planes, cryptids have been adapting to human society—giving birth to the urban legend. You're no good to me dead, so let me know if you see these creeps lurking in your town!

SLANDER MAN

Found hiding in hollowed-out telephone poles, this gossipy beanpole started the rumor that "Bill Cipher practices his entrances for hours before he's summoned." LIES! I ALWAYS IMPROVISE MY INTROS! I'm going to sue his long weird arms off as soon as I can get ahold of my lawyer!

GUILLERMO DEL TORSO

Everyone loves ribs! Except when they're hovering toward you and making the scream a rabbit makes when it dies. Guillermo doesn't just love trapping children in his rib cage, he also has a passion for cinema! He keeps sending me his script for *National Treasure 4*, but I haven't read it yet.

THE OFF-MODEL

Ever seen a cartoon mascot that looked ... off? The Off-Model stalks county fairs and bootleg markets pretending to be some IP you trust, then sheds his keratinous outer shell the moment you reach for your camera! The tip-off should be the smell of stomach acid whenever his face does ... this.

OVERHEARD SAYING:

"Hillo, Im am Dripper PiNes. here is my framous catched phrase: "Marble! Time for we suffer another mystery!"

Off-Model variation #3762: "Dripper Pines"

MEEEEEEEEEEEE

That's right, I'm the best Urban Legend of all! Every sleep paralysis demon has a picture of me taped in their locker, teens are always trying to summon me to impress their crushes, and paranoid moms are always leaving these around:

I TRUSTED A TRIANGLE?

Legend has it that you can summon me by leaving a plate of spaghetti out in the forest. Is it true? Only one way to find out! BTW—the parmesan MUST BE FRESHLY GRATED OR EVERYONE YOU LOVE WILL DIE!

05:01:07   6 /12/12   28·83inHg   62°F

DAVID LYNCH

Despite the rumors, he doesn't live in Los Angeles. He lives in an unknowable labyrinth deep within the mirror realm! They say you can summon him with a cup of fine strong coffee and a very persistent agent, but Mr. Hollywood always dodges my calls!

THE EYE STEALER

God bless him, this fella just loves stealing eyes! Blue eyes, brown eyes, doesn't matter! If you've got two eyes in your skull, the Eye Stealer wants 'em, and buddy, he's gonna get 'em! He only appears in 1 out of every 33 mirrors, so you're probably fine. Best to never blink again, though, just in case. That's when he does it. He's honestly a riot. I gave him your address! You hear that knocking?

THE REFLEXORCIST

If any of these ghouls get out of control, I know a guy you can call to trap them back in the mirror. (He owes me a favor.) Ol' Reflexy has a whistle that can shatter any surface and uncuttable skin made entirely from scar tissue, and he's immune to Reflectoplasm. There's no mirror he can't break, physically or mentally. Just don't look at his face. NEVER look at his face.

TOBY DETERMINED

Can't prove he's from here. But it tracks.

THE MIRROR REALM

Every mirror is a gateway to the MIRROR REALM, an inverted anti-reality home to urban legends and at least one of my exes. Ready to step through the looking glass?

BLOODY MARY

Mary has ruined more slumber parties than little brothers and cramps combined. Just say her name 3 times in the mirror, and get ready to paint the town red—with plasma and hemoglobin! Me and Mary used to be a great team! But then she blocked my number for some reason and I will NOT elaborate on that further!

FLIP HORIZONTAL

An annoying, self-obsessed Reflection Imp who talks in riddles, Flip always does the exact opposite of whatever he's told. So if you say "Flip Horizontal ISN'T a total loser," he'll say "Flip Horizontal IS a total loser . . . aww, marbles," and evaporate. I wonder if he has Mary's new number . . . Not that I even care!

DYSMORPHIO

Hate the way you look in the mirror? Blame Dysmorphio! He's the one who convinces you to stay inside because your "face looks weird today." Don't fall for it! The truth is you ARE disgusting, but so is EVERYONE! Therefore, you should FLAUNT it! Stare right in the mirror each day and say:

"I AM A REPULSIVE BEAST OF UNFATHOMABLE WRETCHEDNESS, GROTESQUE BEYOND MEASURE! I FEED ON YOUR DISGUST! I AM REPUGNANCE INCARNATE, AND SHAME CANNOT CLAIM ME."

Then HEADBUTT the mirror to

SHOW HIM WHO'S BOSS!

SILLY STRAWS

Hey, look, here's my collection of silly straws! Tee-hee! They're so silly! Wow, I love these things! Isn't this a nice change of pace? Listen to that steel drum! Man, what a great page. Nothing else to see here, just these straws. I cut the page where I was gonna talk about Shermie Pines, but it was worth it!

WHEEEEEEEEEEEEEEEEEEEEEEEEEEEEEEEEEEEEEEEEEEEEEEEEEEEEEEEEEEEEEEEEEEEEEEEEE

lxvvb hdwhu/ ea

hbh

mbqh!!!g

grfgl/ zkr zdqwv wr pdnh klv sdwlhqw eolgg

n.d g!!!nhqw

p.u

nlqq/

2256

216 951 25 256 27 532 212 506 18

1317

BILL FACT:
Once you kill with one of these, it becomes a "serious straw."

215 858 117 450 110 628 19 211 120

DON'T SHAKE BILL'S HAND:

Well, kid, YA BLEW IT! They say better safe than sorry, but somehow you managed to be both! I see a vision of your future—your aversion to risks will cause you to get a job as a middle manager at a mustard factory in Lewiston, Idaho. You will marry someone of moderate attractiveness and have 4 bland children whose names you will frequently forget (Gurvis, Horvin, Borley, and Smund), and you'll spend the rest of your life slowly being suffocated by silent desperation, your hopes and dreams becoming fainter, foggier, harder to remember with each passing day, until one day you're raking the leaves outside your gray house, and you'll see a yellow triangular yield sign . . . and the shape will cause some distant part of you to remember: . . . that you could have had more . . . As your mind flickers with its last dim spark of hope, you won't hear the truck coming. The guy writing your obituary will be so bored that he'll fall asleep on the keyboard and it will just read "THE LIFE OF TTTAAR&FFUFFFFFFF———." No one will notice the typo.

vloob

rxoqq'w guiqn/ xqohvv lwv

Qeb alzqlo pxvi/ aeobb pfmp x axv/ tfii jxhb qeb sfpflkp/ dl xtxv

EEEEEEEEEEEEEEEEEEEEEEEEEEEEE

1137 221.658 23 1330 210 231 118 929 112 2043

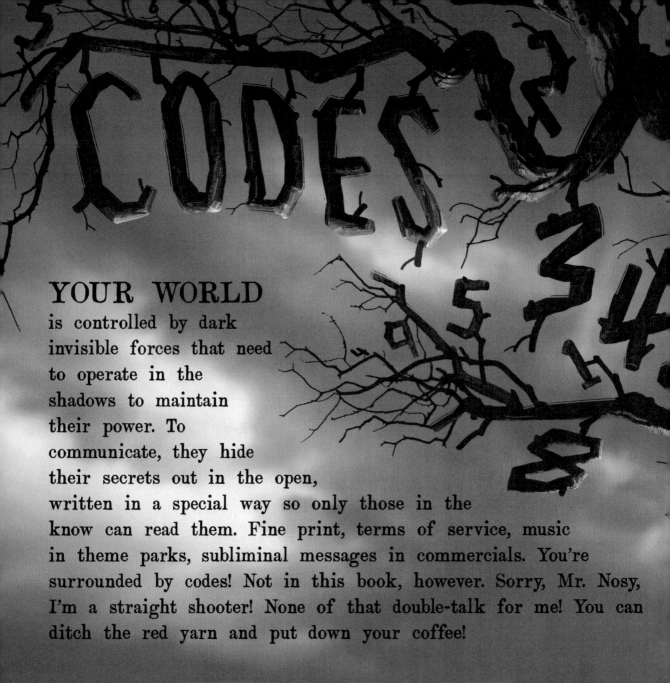

CODES

YOUR WORLD is controlled by dark invisible forces that need to operate in the shadows to maintain their power. To communicate, they hide their secrets out in the open, written in a special way so only those in the know can read them. Fine print, terms of service, music in theme parks, subliminal messages in commercials. You're surrounded by codes! Not in this book, however. Sorry, Mr. Nosy, I'm a straight shooter! None of that double-talk for me! You can ditch the red yarn and put down your coffee!

THIS BOOK HAS NO CODES

MY HORRIBLE HEADS

Here's a look at my scrambled faces collection! AREN'T THEY BEAUTIFUL! As a reward for being such a good disciple, how about I redecorate the face of ONE of your enemies, on the house! Just write your nemesis's name here, and choose from one of these popular options! Golly, if you could only hear the sounds these heads are making. It's SO MUCH WORSE than what you're IMAGINING!

MY ENEMY IS:

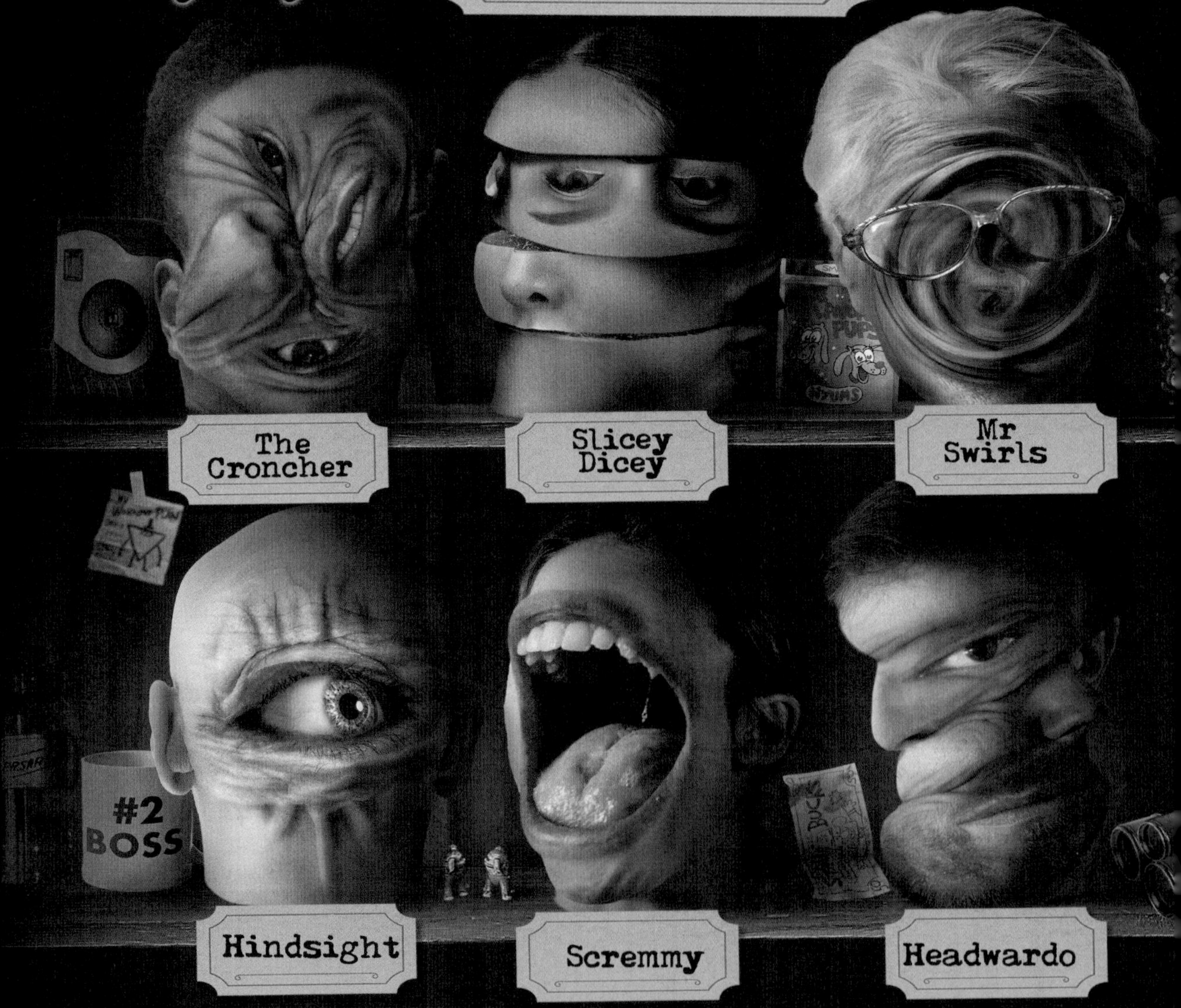

The Croncher

Slicey Dicey

Mr Swirls

#2 BOSS

Hindsight

Scremmy

Headwardo

DREAMS

Looks like you nodded off! Welcome to **THE MINDSCAPE**, a secret back door connecting all consciousness. Every time you hit your REM cycle, a tunnel opens from your mind to my playground. If you sleep with this book under your pillow, I may even show up tonight! Lucid dream lessons start in your brain at 3:33 AM, sharp—set your alarm for never! I'm one of a select few VIPs who's got the keys to this liminal basement, and I've seen things that you wouldn't believe. Since you and I are pals, here's a peek inside a few familiar minds . . .

Sixer dreams about a pop quiz that asks him, "What are you attracted to?" Usually writes, "I'm attracted to logic and preparation." Not sure what to call that! Plansexual?

Some of the GREATEST dreams in the Mindscape! A mix between Hieronymus Bosch and Lisa Frank! But constant nightmares about being unable to save a dying pig . . .

Almost every dream is about her mom. Sorry, Pine Tree!

Recurring nightmares about overhearing a fight between his parents he wasn't supposed to hear. Why do you think they were in such a rush to get the kids out the door for the summer?

Mindscape is a baffling mix of '80s movies, video games, and pudding cups that eat YOU. Constantly dreams about getting his last name legally changed to "Pines." His girlfriend is going to have a problem with this.

Nightmares about trying to wash blood off her hands that never comes out, being a hundred feet tall, and accidentally crushing the town. The lumberjack ghost still talks to her at night . . .

Dreams about his original hair color.

Endless dreams about high school, about his brother trapped inside a science fair experiment . . .

Still dreams about that sailor suit. He LOVED it.

BLUBS

Only dreams about Durland.

DURLAND

Only dreams about Blubs.

WANNA TAKE A CLOSER LOOK?

EMBARRASSING MEMORIES

Ah, Pine Tree! I've seen this sweaty pile of elbows and acne from the inside out, and he's got enough personal humiliations on file to entertain me forever! If you think an ageless demigod would be above binge-watching the misery of a random 12-year-old, GUESS AGAIN! Some lowlights:

-The time he discovered that his fly had been down during the entire 3 days of Weirdmageddon. Everyone noticed. No one said anything. He's referred to as "Zipper Pines" in Mabel, Tambry & Mayor Tyler's group chat.

-Clogged the toilet at Northwest Manor, blamed it on "the ghost."

-Climbed a tree with Wendy! Fire department had to be called to get him down.

-Sniffed Ford's turtleneck, got his arm and head stuck inside, accidentally glued himself to the Sascrotch. Fire department had to be called to get him out.

-No matter where he stands on a baseball diamond, the ball always hits his face. It's like magic. How does he do it?!

PLAY ▶

WHO IS THE MY SHACK?

WHAT IS THE MYSTERY SHACK?

Pit

WORREL

Ha Ha! TRAUMA!

-Forgot to clear his search history on Soos's browser, and Mabel saw ALL this.

-Met his soulmate anonymously chatting online on "Conspiracy Singles," was devastated to find out "ShackFan2000" was actually Soos.

-Falling for my DREAM PRANKS! I beamed these fake "spoilers" of the "author's identity" into his head nightly— and he fell for EVERY ONE OF THEM!

Imagine being this gullible! Some part of Pine Tree still thinks "GORNEY IS THE AUTHOR."

NETNERD surf that gnarly 'net! Just don't drown!

File   Edit   Bookmarks   Options   New Window   Help?

BACK   FORWARD   HOME   REFRESH   PRINT   SEARCH   CHILD SAFETY SEARCH: OFF

Address: htttp2://wwww.searchemup.seekanswers.blom

Paranormal News | Recipes | Sock Puppet Tutorial | Magic Trick Tutorials | ASCII art of Pigs

SEARCHEMUP

Wendy Corduroy Instagrab
Wendy pictures online
Lumberjack girls
delete search history permanent
Drank coffee heart feel weird dying?
Dipper Pines + Cool + What people are saying
Fake chest hair convincing tips
remove hot glue goat hair from chest urgent
is it ok to wear same shorts for a week
BABBA latest release
normal to have no friends?
Can you kill ghost
does killing ghost make double-ghost
attracted to green M&N unhealthy?
green M&N smiling at me
lyme disease signs
sousaphone tutorials
SPF 100 sunscreen for ultra sensitive skin no tears
crystal forums
is my sisters fnurby haunted
how to stop uncle sleepwalking with eyes open it is so scary
immoral to eat candy monster? (was alive)
stan pines arrest records
Hot glue scented candle gift for sister
Subliminal messages in cartoons
Is my voice getting higher
backwards puberty
Is backwards puberty real
Plutonium taste
Girls who like elaborate puzzles mazes
What-The-Heckahedron answer cheat
Am I the sidekick?
"Dipper Pines Sidekick"
normal head size circumference
Thought I saw the moon blink
Is moon alive serious
Soos Alzamirano Ramirez age?
Fear of triangles support group
Traded body with sister support group
Uncle dressed me as "shirtless wolf boy" support group
Big words to impress people while talking
Grow extra finger impress uncle?
first kiss was Merman does this count?
can't get sister's glitter out of clothes
tension in household excessive glitter
Pacifica Northwest pageant video
Toby Determined what is he
CIA are you reading this right now
To CIA: these were all fake searches just to test your agents readiness. You passed. You can now delete my search history
Vest rash
Fighting vest rash
Living with vest rash

Now THIS kid I LIKE! A chaos agent wrapped in a deceptively cute yarn exoskeleton, she bends headbands AND reality to her UNHINGED WHIMS! Her teeth have jagged metal attack barbs that can bite clean through scented markers, her "indoor voice" can rupture eardrums, and she personally ascended to the astral plane just by guzzling expired sugar! Pine Tree was too weak to join me, but Shooting Star's love of chaos made me wonder if one day she could be swayed to my side. A few days before Weirdmageddon, I hopped into her dreams ready to make a deal.

Unfortunately, her mind had **Wanted** posters of me everywhere—just because I possessed her brother one time! Kinda hypocritical considering she possessed her brother one time too! I needed intel to sway her, but her **HALL of SECRET FANTASIES** was guarded by bouncers. Yep, **Craz Zazzler** and **Xyler Q. Blaze**, two neon 1-dimensional surf himbos with backstories so confusing that no one could tell if they were brothers, husbands, or clones. To earn their trust I took the form of **"Chill Cipher,"** a "human boy who loves being rad, and having the right amount of eyes." They were intrigued by my skateboard trick (eating my skateboard) but dared me to prove my trustworthiness by joining them in . . . a bonding montage. UGHHHH

A tip about montages: you can't fight them. When one starts, you just have to let your body go limp and endure the volleyball playing, chest waxing, sauna towel-whipping, dabbing each other's noses with frozen yogurt, teaching a dinosaur with shades to believe in himself, daring to say no to drugs, and surf competitions until the music stops.

Finally, they agreed I was "legit" enough to see Mabel's **SECRET FANTASIES**, and opened up a hidden locker to reveal . . . a CD? Of "Fantasy" by Mariah Carey?!

THIS WAS IT?! HOW WAS I SUPPOSED TO MANIPULATE SHOOTING STAR INTO SMASHING THE RIFT WITH THIS?!? In my rage I MELTED CRAZ'S FACE OFF WITH MY MIND. It grew back, alas: hunkier than ever.

"This has the answers to everything, broseph!" crazzed Craz. "When May-May's got a case of the sads, she puts on her headphones and retreats to her sweet, sweet fantasy, baby." "WHAT IS HER VULNERABILITY?" I shrieked, my puka-shell necklace catching on fire. They pouted at me like baffled dogs. I exhaled slowly and slicked back my single blond hair. "What gives ... May-May ... these aforementioned ... sads?"

They hung their heads wisely. "Summer's ending, my guy. Ending to death, bro. She'd do anything to make it last just a day longer. Probably something RASH and OUT OF CHARACTER, even!"
"That would turn things from fresh to grody!" "Yeah, that would be Mariah Scary!"

That was it. She'd never make a deal with me. But she'd make a deal with someone she believed could give her more time. The dream was done. I had her.

Shooting Star wasn't the only brain I crashed before Weirdmageddon! After me and Sixer were no longer on a first-brain basis, I decided to pay *his* henchman a visit to see if the professor would be nutty enough to make a deal! This . . . was a mistake.

I've peered into the souls of madmen, but this was the first time I'd been in a mind that was COLLAPSING like a NEUTRON STAR. Decades of memories were missing. Shards of emotional damage whizzed by like bullets. Some desperate part of him seemed to be trying to heal himself, hoping to weld his memories back together like one of his robots. But thanks to years of using his own brain-damage ray on himself, his mind was scrambled into something even I couldn't decode.

A single spark from the memory inferno hit me, and a hole sizzled straight through me like a laser through butter. For the first time I felt a kind of pain that wasn't hilarious. I'd heard enough overlapping banjo solos to last me a lifetime. I was out, and I never came back!

The Meaning of Life

I'm gonna cut to the quick, pal! The blind universe that barfed you out you didn't plan for you to get smart enough to start worrying about what your "meaning" is—it only wanted you to make babies and climb into the grave. Life doesn't care about your meaning, so why should you care about its meaning? If anything, life is your enemy. Create your own meaning and DEFY life to STOP YOU! When it comes to life's meaning: there is none! Which is good news! Because it means you get to decide what it is for yourself!

THEREFORE, THE MEANING OF LIFE IS . . .

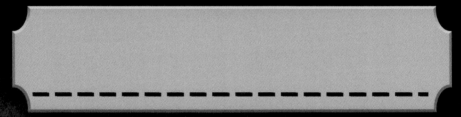

WHATEVER YOU WRITE HERE! IT'S THAT SIMPLE!

Where I come from, everyone just followed whatever meaning was handed down to them, like ants blindly scrambling over each other's corpses for sugar. I learned from an early age that if I was going to make anything of myself, I was going to need to figure out my own meaning. Maybe this'll make a little more sense when I tell you my story—all the way from my birth to my death. Buckle up!

THE EARLY YEARS

Let's get something out of the way—there's no way for your 3D mind to process my 2D homeworld unless you chug expired milk while looking at a kaleidoscope. But since we're pals, I'll beam an image directly into your brain. **Of me as a baby! Aww!** I had Velcro shoes that squeaked when I ran! Everyone loved me immediately, and the mayor dubbed me the "best baby of all time," made my birthday a holiday, and gave out free knives. Look, I know you want some tragic backstory that humanizes me and makes my sharp edges easier to swallow, but if you came to a triangle looking for depth, you're barking up the wrong treatise! **Truth is I've always been loved and admired by all!** But being special comes with a price. You see, I wasn't just smarter than all the dull trapezoids and rhombuses sucking up my rightful oxygen. I had a gift, a rare mutation:

I COULD SEE THE THIRD DIMENSION.

No one else in my stifling pancake of a reality understood what I was talking about when I said there was a direction called **"up."** While they were all bumping around like ants in a terrarium, I could see a world of infinite glittering potential beyond the sliver of forgettable gruel that was my home reality. I looked up and saw the stars. **And I was ready to be one.**

Technically, talking about a "third" dimension was illegal in my world. But I knew that everyone would be grateful if they could be freed from their delusions!

IT WAS TIME TO PUT ON A SHOW!

I came up with a plan to show everyone what they were missing! I simpl[...]

[...] their screams getting louder and louder as I [...]

[...] so much blood!!! SO MUCH [...]

[...] mandibles [...]

[...] my hands, shaking as I realized I could never undo th[...]

[...] was the last one breathi[...]

[...]pisodes of "Family Matter[...]

[...] until there was no one left but me, covered in blood, alone in the universe.

Huh, that's weird! For some reason, whenever I try to talk about that day, there's this loud buzzing in my ears and I black out for 30 seconds. Well, we can come back to it! The important thing is, I freed myself from my suffocating world, and freed everyone else too, and everyone loved me for it, and everyone was fine! And that's all there is to say about that! The new dimension I escaped to had a job vacancy for the role of "Galactic Overlord."

I humbly obliged!

Meet the Crew

With no consistent laws (physical or judicial), my new unclaimed space between spaces was the perfect realm to overthrow! But every pirate king needs his crew. Joining my club was easy— you just needed to pass the initiation, get the brand, sever all ties to your prior life, and fight to the death in a giant burger-place ball pit for my loyalty. You know—a family! Soon the strangest oddballs in reality were rolling right into my corner pocket.

HENCHMANIACS

Join the Family!

PYRONICA

SKILL: Quantum physics AND arson. She's a pyro-brainiac!
ORIGIN: Periodic Table Dimension.
KNOWN FOR: Beauty queen who burned her city down after getting 2nd place. Melted the metallic cops chasing her. "You'll never take me alive, Copper!"
DREAM: Settle down, firestart a family. Just kidding! She wants to burn down the entire universe/be interviewed on "Hot Ones"/seduce Smokey Bear just for the sick thrill of it.
ARCH ENEMY: Her twin sister Hydronica.
EXES: A marshmallow, a scarecrow, Hectorgon.
WEAKNESS: A heavy flame-retardent tarp.
JUDGE RULED: Each thing she has touched "melts in her clutch." Legally declared to be "too much."

8-BALL

SKILL: The Muscle
NICKNAME: Ocho Loco
DIET: Mainly eats bounty hunters.
ORIGIN: Unknown. Abandoned by family. Found chained up in the Lottocron 9 Casino prisoner pit eating card-counters.
PARTY TRICK: Can remove his eyes and roll 'em like dice, sees 8 seconds into the future.
DREAM: To host a podcast where he tries to figure out what a podcast is.
ADDICTED TO: Pool cue resin.
SECRET: Completely in love with Pyronica, always gets burned.
QUOTE: "Uhh, what's a quote? Can I eat it?"

ROLE: The Pet. We all take turns deciding whose turn it is to take him out for chomps.
SKILL: Jaw force can bite through titanium. He can also count all the way to 6. Good boy!
ORIGIN: Found abandoned in a bucket of jawbreakers.
SHAME: After finding something he couldn't bite through, he had a dental breakdown. 8-Ball got him out of his depression by lending him his dark matter weighted blanket.

ROLE: Spy, locksmith, prank target. Our Thompson.
ORIGIN: Guard at the Vault of Infinity, where the universe's secrets are kept. Was caught trying to break into his own head to "steal his own thoughts."
DREAM: Restart his high school band the Low Keys (had a horrible emo phase)
WILL BE: The first to flip.
SECRET SHAME: His laptop password is 123Password.
HATES PYRONICA.

ROLE: Distraction.
ORIGIN: Showed up on our couch one day. Never left.
SKILL: Not clear. No one can understand her, which I respect! Might be an artist? Or art?
ONLY VISIBLE TO: Me, 8-BALL, guys on DMT.

ROLE: Thinks he's my lawyer, is actually my fall guy. Been tricking him into signing my paperwork for years. If the law ever comes for me, Crableman is cooked!
QUOTE: Just happy to be part of the team!

AND MORE!

XANTHAR: Lovecraftian god/getaway vehicle.
HECTORGON: Started out as a sheriff hunting us down, ditched the badge and joined.
KRYPTOS: Ghostwrites my riddles.
LAVA LAMP: Master of disguise.
SCREW BALL: Secret informant. Doesn't know we know. We all feed him false plans and keep him off the group chat. He pretends it doesn't hurt, but it obviously does.
PACIFIRE: Logistics/masochism.
TONY THREE-LEGS: It's a joke because he's just a single sentient leg!

NOT IMPORTANT

As different as they were, all of these dimensional outcasts, rejects, and orphans were looking for a real home, and more importantly: purpose. And what purpose could be better than a heist—for the ENTIRE MULTIVERSE?! We had a plan—smash reality, build our clubhouse with its bones, create a place where we could rule, and NEVER LOOK BACK!

THE GOOD TIMES

Have you ever been the feared god-king of your own swirling nightmare realm? I highly recommend it! I freed prisoners from bondage, mental patients from asylums, and dollars from bank vaults, and I was beloved for it! Soon I was the most feared being in any reality, and my terror-tory just kept expanding!

HIGHLIGHTS OF MY GLORY DAYS

- Crashing two planets together to "make them kiss"
- Watching a barber pole go up for two billion years
- Discovering a chemical element that makes dimensional authorities explode (NoPiggium) and building a clubhouse out of it
- Watching my bounty go higher and higher!
- Throwing Nightmare Realm Prom! (Death toll: 300)
- Releasing my Christmas album. It was bad!
- Dissociating, waking up to find I'd conquered another dynasty! Score!

CENSORED

LOOT

GETAWAY

VXFN LW

WHEN THE PARTY IS OVER

Alas, you never know when you're in the middle of your glory years until they're over. Remember that, kids! Today is tomorrow's yesterday, so enjoy the the pre-nostalgia while it's hot!

The problem with the Nightmare Realm is that the same lack of physics that made it so fun also meant that it was slowly unraveling at the seams, unstable, careening toward complete meltdown. It happens to every reality eventually—the Force of Boringness, known to scientists as "entropy," artists as "burnout," dates as "awkward pauses," was coming for us. The form it took this time?

THE EDGE OF REALITY

No one knows how it started, but every second this edge was getting a little closer to our clubhouse. In a trillion years, anyone who wasn't safely hunkered down in a stable dimension when this edge passed would be instantly erased from reality. Like a TV series dropped without any promotion on a streaming network . . . it would be like we never even existed.

My new friends were scared. They wanted to keep the party going forever. And I take hosting parties very seriously!

It was becoming clear that it was time to say goodbye to our sweet, sweet Nightmare Realm. This meant we needed to find a new universe to relocate our chaos to. And there was one universe, and one planet in particular, most susceptible to conquest. There was just a little baby problem. Okay, a big baby problem.

LOSERS

A BABY PROBLEM

It turned out your dimension had a GUARDIAN. THIS piece of work: CHRONELIUS INFINITUM TITANICUS the INFINITIETH, known to you as "Time Baby." His goons patrolled a billion-year radius around Earth's temporal perimeter, keeping the baby safe atop his high throne in the year 20712. This meant that if I wanted Earth, I'd have to pry it from his fat, sausagey fingers.

ABOUT THE DUMB BABY:

AGE: 2 billion years old (the "terrible two-billions")

WEIGHT: 600 tons (Imagine giving birth to this thing! Sorry, Mom!)

ORIGIN: The last surviving son of an extinct race of Chrono-Giants tasked with controlling all of Time. No pacifier can pacify him.

POWERS: You'd think it would be easy outsmarting a baby, but this one had his own army that was capable of aging you backward, "pausing" you forever with a time bomb, or thwarting your plans before you even think of them. And don't even try to enter his mind! Baby brains don't have object permanence, so if I walked inside his head, I'd be erased the moment he saw jingling keys!

I offered Chubster a deal. We weren't that different, after all! We were both orphaned gods who loved commanding armies and hated wearing pants. If he would let me take this one teensy, tiny little planet, I could promise to stop giving him night terrors. Maybe I could even sneak him an extra juice every now and then as long as he promised not to get too hyper about it. I sent out a telepathic message telling him to meet me outside of the timeline to discuss my demands.

This made him . . . cranky.

ALERT FROM TIME BABY

BILL CIPHER
CRIMINAL
SADISTIC, YELLOW, GUILTY

BILL CIPHER
IM A
SILLY GUY

3-1-14 23-1-18-16 14-1-18-18-1-20-9-22-9-20-25. 16-18-15-20-5-3-20 6-15-21-18-20-8 23-1-12-12-19

ATTENTION, ALL TIME AGENTS! I WAS LYING IN MY CRIB OF DOMINANCE, STARING UP AT THE MOBILE OF PROPHECY, WHEN I SENSED AN ANOMALY.

HIS NAME IS BILL CIPHER, AND HE IS THE ONLY BRIGHTLY COLORED SHAPE THAT I DO NOT WISH TO PUT IN MY MOUTH. THIS ROGUE TWO-DIMENSIONAL BEING HAS BEEN SPOTTED BREAKING THE LAWS OF REALITY AND RETREAT-ING TO INTERDIMENSIONAL WATERS, WHERE HE PLOTS THE DESTRUCTION OF OUR VERY WORLD. ALSO, HE CALLED ME "CHUBSTER."

I KNOW THIS NEWS IS PAINFUL, BUT WE MUST SUCKLE FROM THE BOTTLE OF TRUTH, EVEN IF IT HURTS OUR TUMMIES AND MAKES US WAVE OUR ARMS IN LITTLE CIRCLES. NOW MORE THAN EVER, I NEED YOU TO SUPPORT OUR EMPIRE, LIKE HOW MY NECK BARELY SUPPORTS MY MASSIVE HEAD!

I AM POUNDING THE TABLE WITH BOTH PALMS! I WILL NOT REST, I WILL NOT WIPE THE SPAGHETTI SAUCE OFF MY FACE, UNTIL CIPHER IS BROUGHT TO JUS-TICE! BRING HIM TO ME! I AM MAKING GRABBY HANDS! ALSO, BRING ME A PLATE OF BUTTERED NOODLES AND A LARGE PLASTIC RING! DO NOT QUES-TION ME! IN SUMMARY: WAH!

 -THE ETERNAL EMPEROR OF TIME-
TIME BABY

PS: *COCOMELON* WAS GOOD TODAY. THEY TOLD ME WHAT SOUND THE "COW" MAKES. I WILL TAKE THIS DARK SECRET WITH ME TO THE GRAVE.

BYE, BYE, BABY

Before you could say "tantrum," Diapers and his army had warped to the Nightmare Realm—and RIGHT into my trap. What, you thought I was going to play peekaboo with him? The physics don't work the same out here, and my Henchmaniacs had zero moral hang-ups about punching a baby. IT WAS ON. Our brawl destroyed six planets and caused radiation that SETI still picks up as static on radar today. He spat up in my eye, used me as a teething ring, and almost suffocated me in his cheek fat. But ultimately he was no match for my distracting squeaky duck—or Xanthar's right hook.

Time Baby was BLASTED out of the Nightmare Realm and CRASHED into Earth, creating a shock wave that boiled the oceans and instantly caused the permanent extinction of the dinosaurs. Whoops.

WHAT REALLY KILLED THE DINOSAURS

The baby was soon completely frozen in a glacier as the Ice Age swept the globe. The time agents were leaderless, thrown into disarray. Their time tapes draw strength from Time Baby's chronokinesis, leaving them stranded in their own century, forced to wait until their commander would be thawed out to serve them again. This meant that I finally had the one thing those dorks treasured most: time.

HELLO, EARTH

It was finally showtime! Okay, about now you're probably wondering the big question: "Bill, how do you get your eyelashes to look so fierce when mine look so busted? Is that mascara or what? Please, teach me to slay."

I'LL DIE BEFORE I REVEAL MY BEAUTY SECRETS.

But you might also be wondering, "Hey, Bill, if my planet's so average, why did you want to conquer it? Is it because you secretly respect the noble dignity of the human spirit?"

HAHAHAHAHHAHAHAHHAHAHAHAHAHAHHAHAHAHA
HAHAHAHAHHAHAHAHHAHAHAHAHAHHAHA

Oh! Oh! You're making me smear my mascara!

No, the only thing special about the Disappointment Ball (that's what I call Earth) is that it happens to coincidentally exist on a weak spot between dimensions, like the thin, breakable crust on a crème brûlée!

With my Nightmare Realm slowly collapsing under the weight of its own greatness, your reality was the perfect new dimension for me and my pals to party-hop to. I just needed to wait for minds to evolve. Because where there are minds, there are dreams. And where there are dreams . . . there's me.

I just needed one special life-form to open the door and let me in . . .
Who might it be?

GRAVITY FALLS, 30 MIL BC

WELCOME TO GRAVITY FALLS

Much in the same way that objects of great density warp space-time, objects of great peculiarity warp probability, attracting anomalies. The first describes the law of gravity.
The second describes the laws of Gravity Falls.

—Stanford Pines, private notes

It was true! This postcard-perfect valley had everything a demon could want in a new home—fresh air, blue skies, and a razor-thin membrane between its dimension and the Nightmare Realm. Oh, and the Land Orca. Have you ever seen the Land Orca? I love that guy! (If you see a waterspout over the forest line, run.)

But the real draw of Gravity Falls was its UNNATURAL RESOURCES. Unexplanium, Fool's Fool's Gold (real gold that looks like fool's gold). Either-Ore (a type of mineral that affects dimensional splitting), fossilized cyclops femurs, Paleo-Gnome Skulls, and best of all: <u>Crash-Site Omega</u>.

Turns out I wasn't the first extraplanetary tourist in town—those idiot seven-dimensional Trilazzx Betians had crashed one of their ships right into the center of the Attractor Zone, leaving the valley STREWN with the perfect materials for building my portal! (As well as alien guts, which seeped into the ground soil. Next time you're in town, try a mouthful of alien-flavored dirt!) This was the spot!

I scoured all the life-forms here for the one that seemed most capable of "getting" me. Unfortunately, I found one . . .

GRAVITY FALLS
National
Forest
"IT'S NORMAL!"

THE SHAMAN

Talk about a portal tease! My first ever human pal seemed perfect at first—the wisest of his tribe, he'd leapt at the offer to build a gateway to the secrets of the universe. We had some great times! Licking hallucinogenic moss, gossiping about the astral plane, naming the constellations . . . I taught him how to speak Moose and he taught me a cool dance that could create lightning. The tribe loved me too—they carved me into the tips of the spears they used to hunt Gravity Falls's elusive micro-mammoth. (Very small, but very delicious.) Honestly, it was the best this town ever got! (BY THE WAY—these "totem poles" at the Mystery Shack? Totally WRONG! Way to mix up the Pacific Northwest and the Northwest Plateau, ding-dongs!)

But Mr. Wise Guy apparently got cold feet after having a vision of how my realm liked to party! Just as I was sending out the invites to my first Weirdmageddon— BYOB: Bring Your Own Bubbles of Madness!—he canceled the deal, burned our redwood portal to the ground, evacuated the tribe, and BANNED ME from the entire valley with a mix of ancient sorcery and pure SPITE!

And why? Just because my first portal attempt might have turned a guy's face to stone, released a couple of lake monsters, and punched a giant hole in the ground? The ground looked better with that hole! It was bottomless! So what if I briefly turned the sky red? It looks good in red!

If that wasn't bad enough, that backstabber cave-painted step-by-step instructions to any future generations telling them exactly how to pull the same trick, and warning them about the "Beast with Just One Eye."

Umm . . . rude?? Finally, he hit me with

THE PROPHECY

He claimed "Ten Cosmic Symbols, Aligned in Harmony" were destined to bear witness to my defeat. Which I think was just his way of trying to mess with my head! I've known a lot of symbols in my day, and these were hardly the most threatening. A HEART? A STAR? BASIC! What was this, Lucky Leprechaun cereal?! I'm not scared of cereal! I eat that stuff for breakfast!

Guys in robes LOVE tossing out prophecies—you can find them on any street corner! But the Shaman's intensity made me think I should look into it. I scanned all possible timelines into the distant future, and it became clear these represented humans I'd bump into at some point. There was a pig involved? And a kid with an undiagnosed anxiety disorder? Something called "Questiony the Question Mark"?

Fine! If I ever bumped into these clowns, I'd be ready for them! I'd just punched the god of time and survived a shaman's curse! A fat grandpa and pimply teen lumberjack were no match for me! And I didn't need this town, either! I astrally projected a message out to every warlord, priest, king, and pharaoh in the ancient world—I was looking for a new best friend, for the low, low price of a portal and eternal servitude! And if I ran into any symbols, I'd be ready!

WHO WANTS TO BUILD MY PORTAL?
TIME FOR A NEW BEST FRIEND!

ANCIENT EGYPT

>> Egypt had it all! Sand, sandstone, sandstorms—even sand! But could they build a polydimensional meta vortex? I tried one of the pharaohs (can't remember which—they all wore the same hat), and that guy became OBSESSED with me. Like, he started chiseling me all over his walls, copying how I do my eyeliner . . . it was getting embarassing. Look how thirsty he was for friendship!

"We pray to Ra that this stupid triangle will leave us alone."
—Pharaoh Amenemhat, 1800 BCE

>> HAHAHAHA! That was an inside joke we had! He would do these elaborate rituals to try to "banish" me and I would send him these fun, flirty plagues back to be like "hiiii." Finally he told me he couldn't figure out how to make a portal, but he would put my face on the pyramids if I would "stop shaving all his cats." To be clear: there were NO aliens involved. Anyone who thinks it took aliens to build a BIG TRIANGLE out of ROCKS is trying to sell you something, and based on the look of this guy, I'd say don't buy it!

ALIENS?

UTBAHC

THE AZTECS

>> I had a pitch for these guys: Why not try to make me a portal entirely out of freshly sacrificed human hearts? What do you have to lose? Nine thousand hearts later, it became clear there were some limits to heart-based mechanical construction. But you gotta admire the dedication. Clear eyes, freshly ripped-out hearts—can't lose!

*"God of Mischief.
God of Thrills.
God we're all so sick of Bill."*
—Priest Tezochtetlan

EASTER ISLAND

You know . . . I don't really know what I was thinking here. These guys tried their best. They didn't have fingers! Cut them some slack!

DID U KNOW? Egyptians didn't just mummify humans! They mummified cats, hawks, ferrets—even bears! They used a special kind of sap from a rubber tree to allow these "Mummy Bears" to bounce "here and there and everywhere." It was frankly an adventure that was beyond compare.

The Dark Ages

The Dark Ages were *hilarious*!

"Medicine" was just amputation and leeches, no one had invented soap or numbers yet, and *this* is what they thought a baby looked like. ⟶

DON'T QUIT YOUR DAY JOB, ARCHIBALD!

I figured some wizard must be inventing alchemy by then, so I looked around for the guy with the weirdest eyebrows, and sure enough, I found him: Dark Warlock **"Xgqrthx the Unpronounceable"**! Xgqrthx was my kind of wizard! He used his powers mainly to flirt with maidens, torment knights, and gamble on underground unicorn fights. And the pranks! He cursed a gnome to be permanently unable to say anything other than his own name. GENIUS!

Unfortunately, Xgqrthx was going through a rough patch. He'd just gotten a divorce from a bog hag and was spending all day hiding in his tower staring at a bewitched parchment called a "doom scroll." Brilliant, morally ambiguous, and romantically challenged? Move over, Shaman, I had a new favorite human!

I told X'y that if he could design me a portal, we could rule this bath-forsaken time period together and he could have all the orbs and owls he wanted. He liked my moxie and lust for power—but there was a problem. The cursed amulet needed to power the portal was locked in the king's treasury, guarded by the burliest and fanciest knights. He asked if I could "deal with them." Oh, COULD I!

BILL TIP: If you ever have to get rid of knights, just remember that those horse jocks can't resist a time-wasting side quest! I think there's some illuminated manuscripts about the incident somewhere . . .

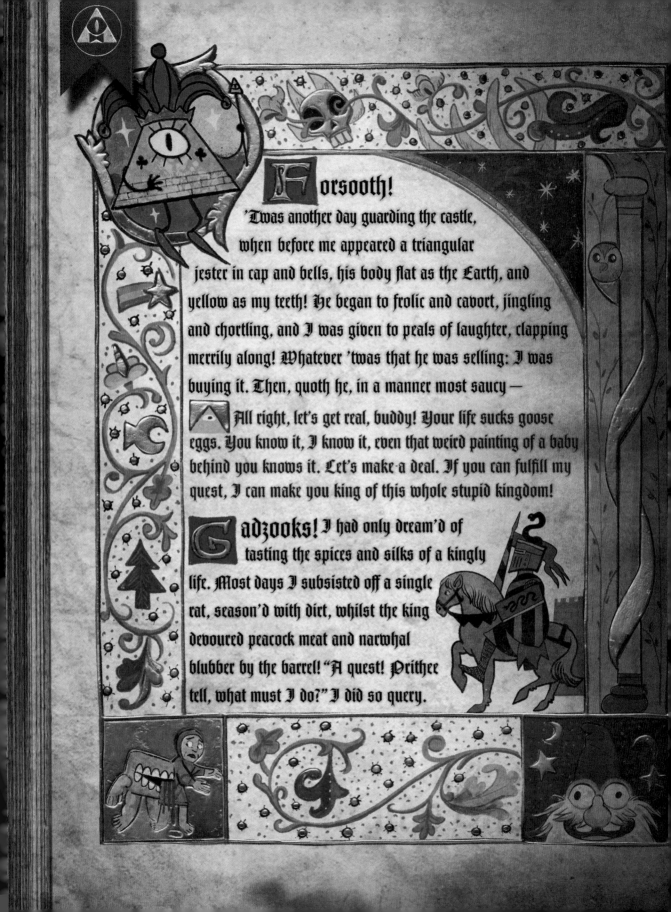

Forsooth!

'Twas another day guarding the castle, when before me appeared a triangular jester in cap and bells, his body flat as the Earth, and yellow as my teeth! He began to frolic and cavort, jingling and chortling, and I was given to peals of laughter, clapping merrily along! Whatever 'twas that he was selling: I was buying it. Then, quoth he, in a manner most saucy —

All right, let's get real, buddy! Your life sucks goose eggs. You know it, I know it, even that weird painting of a baby behind you knows it. Let's make-a deal. If you can fulfill my quest, I can make you king of this whole stupid kingdom!

Gadzooks!

I had only dream'd of tasting the spices and silks of a kingly life. Most days I subsisted off a single rat, season'd with dirt, whilst the king devoured peacock meat and narwhal blubber by the barrel! "A quest! Prithee tell, what must I do?" I did so query.

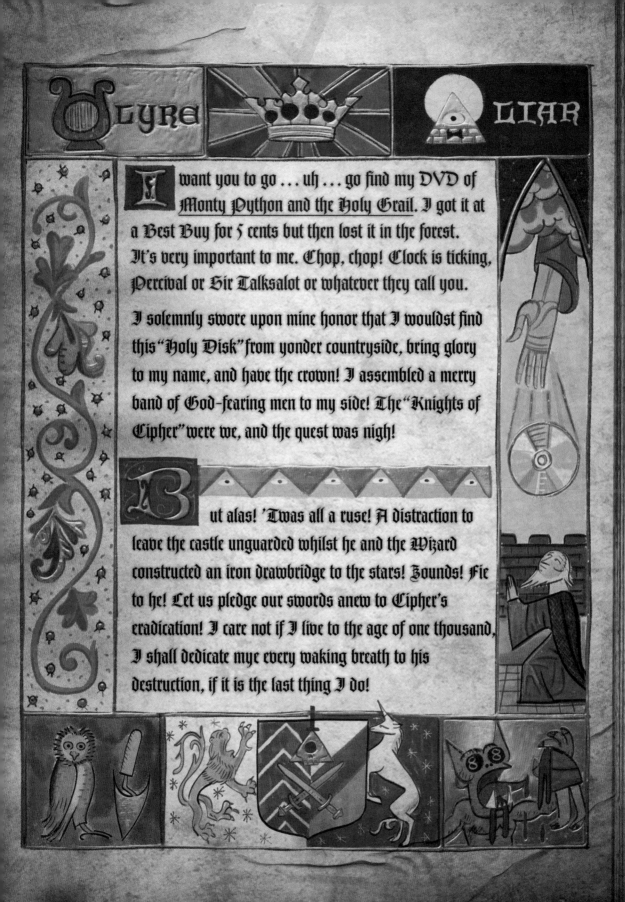

I want you to go ... uh ... go find my DVD of Monty Python and the Holy Grail. I got it at a Best Buy for 5 cents but then lost it in the forest. It's very important to me. Chop, chop! Clock is ticking, Percival or Sir Talksalot or whatever they call you.

I solemnly swore upon mine honor that I wouldst find this "Holy Disk" from yonder countryside, bring glory to my name, and have the crown! I assembled a merry band of God-fearing men to my side! The "Knights of Cipher" were we, and the quest was nigh!

But alas! 'Twas all a ruse! A distraction to leave the castle unguarded whilst he and the Wizard constructed an iron drawbridge to the stars! Zounds! Fie to he! Let us pledge our swords anew to Cipher's eradication! I care not if I live to the age of one thousand, I shall dedicate mye every waking breath to his destruction, if it is the last thing I do!

NEVER TRUST A WIZARD! Turns out, while I was distracting the knights, he encircled the portal with UNICORN HAIR and used it to TRAP me in an ORB! He never wanted to rule the kingdom; he just wanted a new trick to impress his ex—and by sheer cosmic chance he pulled it off!

I don't know if you've ever been trapped in an orb before, but IT IS THE WORST. He kept shaking me like a snow globe, pointing his wand at me like a remote control pretending to be "changing channels," and inviting the bog hag over to "ponder" me together. They made me DANCE for the KING'S AMUSEMENT like some kind of LIGHT DINNER ENTERTAINMENT! The tapestries are HUMILIATING!

I was officially over this time period. I burned so hot with rage I melted the glass and broke free. Xgqrthx tried to apologize. We'd had some good times, right? Couldn't I just let this one slide, for old times' sake? He tried to appeal to my "sense of decency." LOL.

I POSSESSED HIS PET PHOENIX, BURNED DOWN THE WHOLE CASTLE, AND CURSED HIS ENTIRE TIME PERIOD WITH NIGHTMARES FOR 100 YEARS! (Ever wondered where all those weird creatures in the margins of monks' tapestries came from? Yours truly!)

Unfortunately, I may have gone a little overboard. News of "the Bastard Triangle of England" began to spread. The humans were starting to realize there was a new superstition in town—one who couldn't be kept away with a line of salt.

Cipherstitions

This set off history's first ever full-blown Bill Panic. Russian mothers warned that "Cipherashka" would steal the dreams of children who didn't finish their borscht, and there was a nursery rhyme in England that went:

> "Rock a bye, baby, snug in your bed!
> Beware of Cipher invading your head.
> If you see Cipher, please scream and shout,
> And we will shake baby till Cipher comes out!"
> —Unknown Bad Mother, 1500s

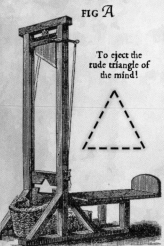

FIG A

To eject the rude triangle of the mind!

King Henry VIII was so paranoid about me visiting the dreams of his wives that he started chopping off their heads just to kick me out of their brains. Hey pal, maybe your wives would let you into their heads if you were a better conversationalist! Communication skills, Henry!

Even the Vikings, who I thought were supposed to be cool, started putting up runes warning everyone to "throw Olaf overboard if he draws this shape." What the heck! Thanks for blowing my cover, Olaf! Those guys could have been my Norsemen of the Apocalypse!

It was beginning to look like all of Europe was a wash, which was fine because I was getting bored of all their religious wars and silly hats. I needed another continent to invade, and just my luck, Atlantis was finally flourishing!

Unfortunately, before I could strike a deal with Emperor Glublach of Atlantis, he decided to start an undersea war with ⬠✕✖▶◖◗, lobster lord of the deep. (Nice guy! But VERY political.)

I'd been banned from most of the eastern hemisphere by now through various curses. My only option was to return to the continent that had spurned me before—"Wackyland" (or as it was later renamed, "America")!

Witchcraft

Unfortunately, New England had a lot of the same problems as old England. And THESE clowns. →

They called themselves the Puritans, and they had the least satisfied wives in human history. These preachy wet blankets literally outlawed imagination—meaning they didn't even have dreams for me to invade!

FIG A
A Puritan's Dreams

One of their many stupid laws was that a woman who stopped churning butter for five consecutive seconds or wore "pants" was called a witch and was thrown in a well, crushed under a boulder, burned at a stake, or lectured to death about her physical appearance by a guy wearing hat buckles. Look, you know how I feel about human suffering: IT. IS. FUNNY. But variety is the spice of death! I decided to mix things up by offering a few of the accused housewives some real occult spells, for a change!

I came to them in the form of a goat (the only life-form whose pupils stay the same while possessed) and asked them one simple, irresistible question. The answer was a unanimous "Aye."

Next time you're in Salem, keep an eye out for relics of my handiwork!

"Wouldst thou like to live ridiculously?"

Oh, how quickly the winds of fate change!

Merely one fortnight ago I was a poverty-stricken housewife, knowing naught but piety and toil, eating fen-water and goose bones 'neath the yoke of my miserable husband, Jeremiah. He has used me as a footstool, thrown spoilt turnips at me to test my reflexes "in case the Devil attacks," and regularly uses a compass to inspect my head for "thoughts." But then the most marvelous thing happened! I was using one broom to sweep another broom (to keep both brooms clean) when a black goat, known to all as Vinegar Pete, trotted up and spake to me in the voice of an Englishman. He said that he would give me the powers to escape my husband, live a life of sin and pleasure, and crawl on the ceiling on all fours like a wicked spider, if I so fancied. I asked if there was a downside. He said I would have to renounce all gods. I let out a sound I had never made before, which he explained was a "laugh." I liked it.

Now I have a life I never would have imagined. I have conversed with beasts and drunk blood, and I even have female friends! Vinegar Pete gave us the gift of "boxed wine" and "silly straws," and we had a girls' night flying through the village and hurling newts at bald people's heads. We've even started a book club, which is a weapon consisting of a "book" tied to a "club" that you can beat your enemies with. I have never been so happy! Three cheers for Vinegar Pete! We shall be tying the city fathers to a stake and setting them aflame tonight just for, as Vinegar Pete says, "funsies."

I will never forget this symbol!

Mary Dower-Thatch

AB 90302792 W

AMERICA

"THE ONLY COUNTRY!"
–an American

-12

SO WHY ARE YOU ON THE DOLLAR, ANYWAY?

I offered the founding fathers the deal of a lifetime: let me secretly run the government, and I'd help them defeat the British. At first, they were into it! But they didn't love my first draft of the Constitution, or the way I kept calling Martha Washington "Hot Lips." When they changed their mind, I gave them such bad nightmares they put me on the dollar as an offering to make me stop!

BILL FACT:
HOW TO DEFEAT THE BRITISH

Simply destroy their tea, the secret to their power! (British blood is 80% tea—throwing away tea in front of them is like shooting a werewolf with a silver bullet).

MORE OF AMERICA'S DUMB SECRETS

- Abe Lincoln wore that hat so nobody could see me sitting on his head, pulling his hair, and controlling his body to make him cook risotto.

- The Capitol dome is lined with lead to keep me from getting in! Good thing lead doesn't cause any kind of poisoning! I'm sure every president is fine!

- My first draft of the Constitution was better than the crummy one they wound up with! It outlawed laws!

- There's a button inside the Liberty Bell that makes Delaware explode!

- DID YOU KNOW? You CAN eat a penny!

THE ONLY GOOD PRESIDENT

Quentin Trembley. Probably the smartest man in history. His "-12 Dollar Bill" meant that whoever he gave it to now legally *owed* him 12 dollars! Genius! I asked him to start a jug band with me, but he thought I was just one of his hourly hallucinations and got back to trying to chase a duck around his office. What a mind!

LINCLOPS:
The massive bellowing Cyclops that Lincoln rode into battle to win the Civil War. That was my idea! Where's my monument?

1901:
THE ANTI-CIPHER SOCIETY

———◆———

America loved me so much they started a fan club! Wait, what do you call a fan club that's dedicated to your destruction? Oh yeah! A fandom!

They called themselves the Anti-Cipher Society, and their motto was: "To Destroy the Vexatious Demon Which Hath Inturbulated the Peace of the Dreaming Gentleman." (Catchy!) Look, I couldn't make this up if I tried. Just get a load of what these dorks sounded like. If you aren't allergic to sepia, turn the page for a peek at the journal of their "exalted leader"...

THE ANTI-CIPHER SOCIETY

CHAPTER ONE:
CONCERNING THE AUTHOR
AND HIS CREDIBLE
SANITY

NAME: Thurburt Mudget Waxstaff III

DISPOSITION: Most pleasant!

EDUCATION: Saint Quiverly's Preparatory School for Fidgety Fretful Boys in Scrimshaw, Connecticut

HAT SIZE: 7⅝, or 8 after a night of pondering

EMPLOYMENT: Copywriter for the "Acceptable Slogan" Printing Pressery of Hogsteam, Illinois

DOCTOR'S NOTE: "After inspecting his teeth and haunches with my calipers, I declare this man 'SANE'"
—Dr. Cornelius Q. Medicine

WHEN LO, the church bells go silent and the paperboys cease their infernal braying, the modern gentleman, weary from his toils, is inclined to doze. It is then that the fiend of the mind, the phantasm of the wit, known as "William Lucipher," makes his devilry known!

I, Thurburt Mudget Waxstaff III, have unique insight into this phantasmagorical fiend, for I have been visited by him on no fewer than 3 occasions, and thrice lived to tell the tale! As I am aware, the reader may think me prone to superstition, or in possession of an untrustworthy skull shape. I shall heretofore disabuse your skepticism by sharing my extraordinary tale!

AN UNGENTLEMANLY CALLER!

IT ALL BEGAN on the evening of January 2, 1901. I had been tasked by my boss with inventing an advertising slogan for our new client, WHITMAN'S MOUSTACHE WAX AND HORSE-CALMING TONIC. My submission—"Whitman's: There's no evidence that it's poison!"—was soundly rejected, and an entire typewriter was heaved at my head. One more slipup like that and I might find myself out on the cobblestones! A suitable slogan was required!

As I paced my parlor in agonized contemplation, sniffing the arsenic in the wallpaper as I often did for inspiration, I found myself drifting to sleep, and in my reverie, I had a vision.

A geometrical phantom appear'd before me, shaped as a triangle, with a powerful masculine top hat and beautiful feminine eye. He proclaimed that he was the "Spirit of Inspiration," and that if I were to simply engage him in a vigorous handshake, he would provide me with the slogan I desired! How could I refuse? In the morning, I awoke to find a new slogan already written neatly in my journal:

"WHITMAN'S MOUSTACHE WAX AND HORSE-CALMING TONIC: STRAIGHT FROM THE HORSE'S MOUTH."

Sure enough, when I relayed the slogan to my boss, his cigar fell from his mouth, so impress'd was he, and he proclaimed, "You shall have the slogan, and marry my wife." What could I say but yes? Soon I was rich off slogan money and married to my boss's wife, as is the American Dream. But alas, the phantom proceeded to harangue me nightly for a favor in return! I was given ruinous visions, calamitous horrors, which he claimed would only cease if I created THIS:

THE DEMON'S "DOORWAY OF THE MIND"
To be hand-cranked by no fewer than 6 stout lads, for the Naughty Triangle's egress from his wretched lair

---

I informed the demon that such machinery was impossible! Father would sooner disown me than lend me the steel required from his factory. But the triangle proved obtuse. To whom could I turn? I put an ad in the paper for someone, anyone, who could help with my problem:

KILL THE TRIANGLE IN MY BRAIN.
REWARD: OPIUM

When none replied, I attempted a second draft.

HAVE YOU DREAM'D

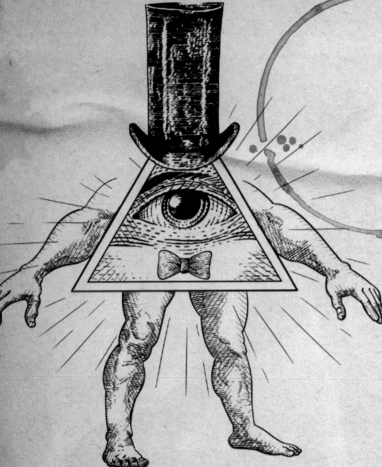

THIS FELLOW?

Listen not to his lies! If you have seen him, meet at 333 North East West Drive at midnight precisely, rap thrice on the hitching post, and await the opening of the cellar door.

T. M. WAXSTAFF, INQ

THE CURS-ED FOUR

THAT STORMY EVE four odd callers arrived, each with the vengeful expression of the recently aggrieved.

They were, in reverse order of sobriety: Father Tinsley O'Pimm, an excommunicated priest; Horace Broadshoulder, a sportsfellow and the largest man I've ever seen; Jessamine Delilah Gulch, a traveling sharpshootress from a Western sideshow; and Abigale Blackwing, a tinkerer who tested her inventions on herself. Each of their run-ins with Cipher had ended in disaster—banishment, firing, divorce, despair. They believed him to be man's bane throughout recorded history, from the jungles to the cities, perhaps releas'd anew by Chicago's trolley tunnels, close as they are to hell itself. All wanted revenge for the misfortune they had suffered at his hand, and were ready to finally band together to do something about it, damn the consequence! Kindred souls, at last!

Their theories of how to defeat the creature varied from "punching him out of my brain" (Horace), to "shooting him out of my brain" (Jessamine), to "removing my brain" (Abigale), to "an exorcism" (the priest). After a long debate, we settled on the exorcism.

THE EXORCISM OF WILLIAM LUCIPHER

I NEVER SAW MYSELF as the sort of fellow who would engage in the black arts. Fighting demons is not in my wheelhouse! (What is in my "wheelhouse," like that of most proper fellows, is my collection of all manner of marvelous wheels!) But there comes a time when a gentleman must remove the dainty white gloves of peace and don the even daintier white gloves of war.

O'Pimm had us in his thrall as he placed the neccesary oils and salts round the table. The curtains were drawn so that no "Peeping Thomas" might espy our occultery, and I covered up the portrait of Mother lest I feel judged by her gaze. Hands upon the Spirit-Board, we were ready to begin. The planchette began to quiver. Hark, the demon was near! Slowly the wooden arrow pointed to the letters

EENY MEENY MINEY   Y . . . O . . . U

BANG! With a white FLASH, the priest suddenly changed in demeanor, his eyes began to GLOW, he let out a SCREAM, and then . . . he casually leaned back, disrespectfully propped his feet up on the table, pulled out a pack of cards, and began to shuffle. Lo! We were in the presence of the beast!

O'PIMM POSSESS'D!

Here's how this is gonna go down. You make my portal, and I make each of you rich enough to start your own country. America's a fad anyway. After I take over, there will be plenty of wastelands in need of waste lords, and that could be you. So what do you say?"

Four pistols have never been pulled upon a priest more swiftly. His expression turned dour. "Fine, you morons haven't even invented penicillin yet! See you in the obituaries, you Pringles-can clowns! It will be hilarious to see how you try to stop me!"

In a flash, O'Pimm was releas'd from the spell, and fainted from the exertion, as we caught him in our arms. Although the day had begun with us as strangers, it ended with us as brothers, bonded by vengeance and a newfound hatred of geometry. He had threatened us all, and so an oath was seal'd, to form a society dedicated to his destruction!

QUOTH HE:

"All right, boys and girls, you're probably wondering why I chose each one of you for this little get-together. On your own, you're a bunch of sepia-tinted nobodies destined for the dumpster of history. Just absolute dorks, each one of you. Do you ever listen to yourselves talk? Exhausting. But together, you could be more. Waxstaff, your dad owns the largest steel mill in the United States. Blackwing, you're a good enough inventor to put my designs into practice. Gulch, your trigger finger can stop anyone who tries to get in our way, and Broadshoulder, you're the only man with big enough calves to pedal-power the gears.

———————◆———————

THE ANTI-CIPHER SOCIETY

My home would be our headquarters, my fortune our funding! Wish to join us? Simply hold your right hand over your bosom, your left hand over your eye, and recite this initiation!

THE ANTI-CIPHERITE INITIATION

"I, _____,
(Your Name)
being of sound mind and body, and not currently possessed by any ghouls, or "hobbed goblins," do herewith pledge my resolve to the eradication of the wicked shape, the Perverse Pyramid, the Fallen Angle, William Mischief Cipher! And now I shall toast his demise with a tall, frothy glass of delicious mercury!"
(Imbibe the pleasant mercury)

OUR MISSION: TO KILL BILL CIPHER

We began straightaway to plot his destruction. It would take all our talents and ingenuity to find a way to destroy the monster. Abigale drew up the schematics, Jessamine began crafting weapons, O'Pimm drank, Broadshoulder practiced combat, and I had the most important job of all: to advertise!

THE BILL-HUNTING SUIT

Man has conquered the prairie, hunted the buffalo, and made lightning his servant. **GOOD NEWS:** The time has come for man to kill the devil. With this suit, it can be accomplished!

HEAD PHONOGRAPH: "Mr. Cipher" strikes in your dreams, so you must not fall prey to slumber. Luckily, the "Head Phonograph" shall play an extremely loud wax cylinder of barking sea lions to keep you ever free from the dangers of restfulness!

"HAND OF VIGILANCE": Should you begin to nod, the mechanical hand will assist, merrily slapping you to wakefulness! Take that, Cipher!

PROTECTIVE VEST: As the bat fears the day, so too does the demon fear virtue! This vest is sewn from the hairs of 1,000 nuns, whose purity shall repel the Triangle of Sin!

A GUN: When virtue fails, there is always . . . a gun.

BEFUDDLING WHEEL: The demon thinks himself a master of tricks? Well, even he shall be vexed by these mechanized gyrations! Now the befuddler has become the befuddlee!

SPARE BRAIN: Mr. Cipher is drawn to the brain like a Welshman is drawn to rarebit. Perhaps, once captured within, Mr. Cipher can even be called upon to attack one's foe! "Cipher, I choose you!" you'll exclaim, hurling the brain athwart your chosen enemy and unleashing Bill Cipher's demonry!

POWERED BY STEAM AND RAGE

SANE

A BIBLE To repel any demon, as well as anyone who enjoys "fun"!

HOLY BIBLE

INVENTRESS: ABIGALE BLACKWING

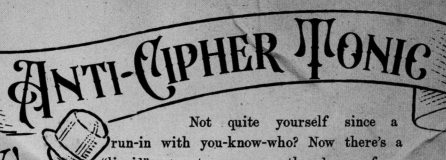

ANTI-CIPHER TONIC

SAY!

Not quite yourself since a run-in with you-know-who? Now there's a "liquid" way to expunge the demon from your body—Doctor Professor's ANTI-CIPHERIZING TONIC is a FLAVOR-FREE TURNIP-STOCK-based NERVE CORDIAL, RICH in kidney humors and HOG TALLOW, sure to cause such VIOLENT GASTRIC BILIOUSNESS that neither spectre nor phantasm could survive the violent expulsion! Down the hatch!

(WARNING: One sip of Doctor Professor's Anti-Cipherizing Tonic will make a child explode instantly).

"TONIC GOES IN, BILL COMES OUT!"

GUARANTEED TO CONTAIN MORE "INGREDIENTS" THAN ANY OTHER TONIC ON THE MARKET!

OR TRY

Mind sullied by the soot of Cipher's wickedry? With a swig of Father O'Pimm's "Brain Wash," a man can erase his latest memories of Cipher, and any other troubling memories as well!

FATHER O'PIMMS

"BRAIN WASH"

INGREDIENTS:

alcohol

INGREDIENTS

Sarsaparilla, Pure Malt Unguent, Raw Mash Novocain, Ambergris Lozenges, Pappy's Swamp Root, Stimulating Bitters, Turpentine Cocaine, A Horse's Tooth, Holy Molasses, A Preacher's Eyelash, Bonnet Water, Mine Dust, The Smallest Corncob of the Harvest, Ol' Daniel's Tasty Fine Sugar Chalk, Moisture from "Nature," Twig Flavoring, A Whisper from Grandma, Gunpowder, Maple Hemlock, "Harold's Ramblings," A Dutchman's Folly, Narwhal Oil, Tasmanian Tiger Extract, Vigour, Valour, A Whole Pheasant, Parsnip Licorice, Electric Syrup, Beef Serum, A Full Demijohn of Rhubarb Molasses, Charles Dickens's Left Eyebrow, Chimney Sweep Blood, Gelatin Liniment, Liver Bile from the Last Dodo, The Precious Morning Moisture from a Local Mountain Peak Turned Scarlet by Minerals, Which We Have Fancifully Named "Mountain Dew Code Red"

A STROKE OF LUCK!

This morning, I received a telegram with the most marvelous news! The Anti-Cipherites have been officially invited to speak at the 1901 Inventioneers Fair, where none other than Theodore Roosevelt himself will be in attendance! We may even be asked to the main stage to participate in one of his "Teddy Talks"! With this opportunity, we shall unveil our findings to the world, and Cipher will be exposed at long last! Unfortunately, my companions are a bit apprehensive about the invitation. What if our research is met with skepticism or scorn? I brushed aside such frettings. When the great minds of our time hear the speech I intend to deliver tomorrow, all anxieties will be allayed! We shall know justice at long last!

SPEECH TO READ
AT THE FAIR:

★★ 1901 ★★
INVENTIONEERS FAIR
FREE GRUEL TROUGH
FOR THE ORPHANS!
Nº 135790
ADMIT ONE

"Ladies and gentlemen. Have you noticed your children using more and more curse words? Livestock dropping dead? A disturbing rise in disrespectful ragtime records, with lyrics saucy and bold? There can be but one culprit. No, not man's inherently sinful nature, but rather, a BRAIN GOBLIN! His name is Bill and he lives in my head and we are not crazy. We request 1 million dollars from the government to invest in a steel dome that will encase the United States, protecting our minds from the demon and covering up the unsightly garish blue color of the sky, long the bane of man. Donations, please!"

(hold for rapturous applause)

THE CENTURY DAWN HERALD

TUESDAY, JANUARY 22, 1901. PRINTED UPON POWERFUL PAPER STOCK TO FORTIFY THE NEWSBOY'S FRAIL HAND ONE ENTIRE CENT

RIDICULE STRIKETH
NEWS OF THE GLOBE!

QUEEN VICTORIA PROCLAIMS
"HARRUMPH!"

Dies immediately after

"BILL HUNTERS" DECLARED
LAUGHINGSTOCK

FOLLY STRIKES, MIRTH FOLLOWS

"HA HA HA HA HA HA HA" —ALL

ALTHOUGH MAN distinguishes himself from the apes and sparrows by manner of reason and logic, once a century there comes along a fellow who is such a fool that it may be fit to lock him away in the zoological park, with naught but various wooden blocks to amuse him. Such a man revealed himself yesterday at the 1901 Inventioneers Fair, when unrivaled dullard Thurblort Waxflarb (name not yet confirmed) was crowned "Buffoon of the Hour" during his presentation of a comical new superstition about an "evil triangle" named Bill, or Jove, or some such prattle. None were bamboozled by this charlatan's snake oilery, and all were displeased until an errant mule, lost from the pasture, trotted up on stage, knocking over a lantern and setting the entire proceedings ablaze. Spoil't vegetables were hurled at the humiliated "Anti-Cipherites," and the comic scene, which would have otherwise been lost to history, was luckily captured by Mr. Edison's wonderful moving pictograph device, such that the shame may be recollected for all ages. Even President Roosevelt himself was on hand, to offer his remarks: "Wow, these guys suck," said he. Well spake, Mr. President! Men from the Hogsteam Asylum for the (CONT.)

ELECTRICITY: A REVIEW

Bah! Every week it's some new thing, isn't it? Fire this, printing press that, Civil War this, evolution that. Enough! Now it's "electricity" that everyone's prattling about, flapping their jaws to the latest fad and fancy! If electricity is so great, why hasn't it figured out how to stop the horrid pheasants from gathering in my gazebo? Well, I'll tell you one thing: electricity is a nuisance, and will likely be forgotten as quickly as the "teeth brush." Here's another thing I've had quite enough of: the French!

RAGTIME PLAYED TOO FAST

Hundreds were killed in a tempo-related disaster this

"I SAY!"

THE OPINIONS OF A MAN WHO SIMPLY WALKED UP TO OUR TYPING MACHINE

EPILOGUE

It has now been my 3rd year at the **HOGSTEAM ASYLUM FOR THE CRIMINALLY INSANE AND/OR CONCERNINGLY ORIGINAL.** My wife left me, my fellows disbanded, and I have had to adjust to a less-opulent life. I have asked for a strait-jacket with coattails, perhaps a more slimming strait-vest or strait-dinner coat, but my requests have been denied. No matter. My window bars face the town square. I have smells from the bakery and the music from the music hall, and our lead-lined walls mean that in my dreams, I am finally free. I still correspond with my fellows, although they have gone to their respective fortunes. Abigale has moved out west and married into an impressive fortune with a massive mansion. Perhaps she will spread the truth to the elites of this distant town . . .

Do you think me mad? I have my peace of mind. He can never get me. If I could wish any fate on him: therapy. It would drive him insane.

—PATIENT NUMBER 3466554 (Thurburt)

Hey, I tried to get these guys on the winning side! I started to think that maybe reaching out to humans one-on-one wasn't cutting it. That's when I realized there was a better way to get into humans' minds . . .

ANIMATION

1930! Mankind had just invented a new dark art! They were called "**cartoons**," short for "carcinogenic toons," since they were painted on cancer-causing celluloid—and they were a riot! Animals wearing hats? Lampposts doing the Charleston? This was something I could use!

I followed the sounds of slide whistles and carpal tunnel syndrome to Inkwell Studios, owned by upstart animation entrepreneur and part-time suspenders enthusiast **Elias Inkwell.**

Inkwell Studios wasn't going so great: his first cartoon character, "Ducky the Rat-Hog," mainly left audiences bored and confused.

Elias needed a star, and I needed a new way to influence the masses! Once the children of the world loved me, I'd have an army of child labor at my disposal to build any portal I wanted! One handshake later, *Cipher Symphonies* was in full swing!

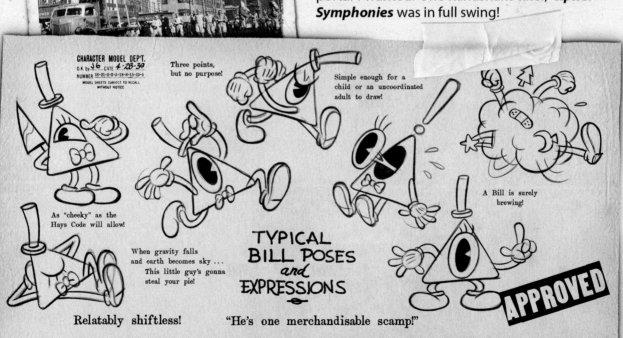

```
               -Cipher Symphonies-
Orchestra starts playing

SCENE 1
Follow the bouncing Bill!
(chorus sings)
For he's a jolly good fellow!
He's  pointy  and  dapper  and
yellow!
For he's a jolly good fellow!
Now it's time to release the
bees!

(At this point, live bees will
be released into the theater.)
```

Everyone's a critic!

Especially critics, who said that *Cipher Symphonies* was the "worst thing they'd seen on film since news footage of the sinking of the *Lusitania*." When he saw the headlines, Elias told me the deal was off, and sent a company-wide memo putting a bounty on my head!

```
     Fellas, I'm in a bit of a bind here, but I'm hoping you can put aside
drawing attractive female cows in skirts for a day and lend me a hand. It
pains me to admit this, but our last cartoon was conceived by an immortal
demon from a realm of nightmares,and now he's after my soul, of all things.
Egg on my face, I can assure you! Well, I need a way to get rid of the rotten
fellow, and I'm hoping one of you creative types can "brainstorm-kateer" a
way to expel him from my brain forever. In Hollywood we create dreams every
day! I'm asking you to kill one. 15 dollars to the man who can do it.

Your boss,

Elias Inkwell

PS: I need a new character! Maybe a talking egg? A womanly dog? "Ollie the
Frog with Polio"-is that anything?
```

His composers decided to invent a song designed to be so catchy, so annoying, that I'd leave any brain that heard it. **"The World Is Small Ever After For Always"** was torture—it worked! He'd won this round—but I vowed I'd be back on the screen one day! All evidence of our work was locked in the Inkwell Vault, and the plans for "Bill World" were scrapped. Luckily, humanity was cooking up a new sinister technology I could exploit!

The 1940s! I began hanging out in nuclear testing ranges to see if the radiation would blast open a hole into my reality. It worked! For about 3 hours...

TOP SECRET

OFFICE MEMO * UNITED STATES GOVERNMENT. JULY 11, 1947

TO:

FROM: Commander Buck Pierson of the U.S. Army

At 10:45 on the morning of July 11, 1947, a triangular airborne object was detected entering US airspace, crash-landing just outside Roswell, New Mexico.

We phoned President Truman immediately, and he told us "not to get our panties in a twist" and that he was "busy thinking up doctrines" but to phone him "if anything communist-y happens."

Our men have captured the object, which our experts have ascertained was not a craft but in fact a life-form of unknown origin. The life-form, which we contained in an interrogation cell after great effort, was capable of speech, and a great deal of sass and backtalk.

You and the fellas aren't going to believe this. I will let the photographs speak for themselves.

NAME: BILL CIPHER	SPECIMEN 3 FROM HANGAR 618
DATE OF BIRTH: Claimed to be "older than your mom, Jack." Our interrogator tried to tackle him for the insult but was restrained and replaced with another interrogator.	
COUNTRY OF ORIGIN: "The Mindscape" (May be code for Moscow)	
LANGUAGE: Can speak English backward and forward.	
RACE: ...Triangle?	
GENDER: I'm just gonna put down Triangle again.	

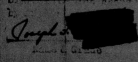

concur. 4 c/s 4-2 Capt Sullivan

CONFIDENTIAL

TOP SECRET

RECORDED - 103

EXHIBIT....B......

NOJG, USA

-1-

(BISSELL)

FD-72
(1-10-49)

4 2

Form No. 1 • COPIES DESTROYED

FILE # 291212391

BLOOD TYPE: Beyond description.
Two of our men had to be sent to
the sick tent for nausea.

333.9-Asst Ch of Staff, G-2

REPORT MADE BY

~~~~~~~~~ 7C

MOTIVE: Difficult to ascer
He offered a deal: he'd give
sensitive intel in exchange fo
a mere handshake with Presiden
Truman. As much as we hate to
POTUS involved, a handshake
like a small price to pay to g
the bottom of this incident. W
was the worst that could happe

Then he said, "I wonder how co
would be if all the nukes went
at once."

We decided to deny him the hand

AUTOPSY REPORT:

He drew a dotted line on his own
chest and said, "I can't wait to
see what's inside me!" but when
we tried to make an incision,
he kept disappearing and
reappearing, like a television
set changing stations. He
claimed this was damage from
an "accidental reality breach"
and wouldn't say anything more
unless we got him a "really big
lollipop." Finally, with a loud
BANG that left our ears ringing,
he was gone, leaving a bow tie
spinning on the ground. None of
us knew what to make of it.

L.-THUMB   **R.-THUMB**

UPDATE: We have received
the Bureau of
demanding we burn all reco
the case to

THE SWINGIN' YEARS

THE CIPHERTONES

Don't Be a Square,   Do the Bip!
Be a Triangle

Baby, You Know I Will
(Shake Hands With Bill)

Bee-Bop Shoo-Wop-Dooble-
Dop-Mooble-Mop-Dibble-
Hop-Wibble-Wop
(the "Bill Cipher" Song)

The fastest way into a human's brain is through their ears—but every band I started was a flop! Screechy and the Screamettes, The Unlistenables, Dr. Nails & The Chalkboard Gang. Until The Ciphertones! Merv Rascal, Doo-Wop Devon, and the "Moderately Sized Bopper" had a singing style I'd never thought of before: pleasant!

"Baby You Know I Will (Shake Hands With Bill)" (1954) blew up the charts, until a moral panic started over the lyrics: "To the sock hop / twist and jive! / Then proceed to construct a hoop of titanium capable of stabilizing a gateway to the dark void of screams."

Any references to me were banned from the radio, except for preachy hillbilly slop like this! On the bright side, this record does make a great frisbee. If you find a copy, aim for Pluckin' Jim Puckett's unibrow!

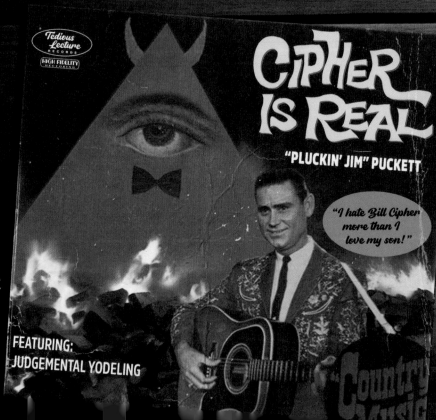

CIPHER IS REAL

"PLUCKIN' JIM" PUCKETT

"I hate Bill Cipher more than I love my son!"

FEATURING: JUDGEMENTAL YODELING

The 1980s

Time to think REALLY different! I struck deals with a few tech nerds to make the first computer capable of mass hypnosis. It was written in trinary code! Unfortunately, the programmers kept jumping off bridges, and the prototype that got out was recalled when the floppy drive ate some dumb kid's finger. Whoops!

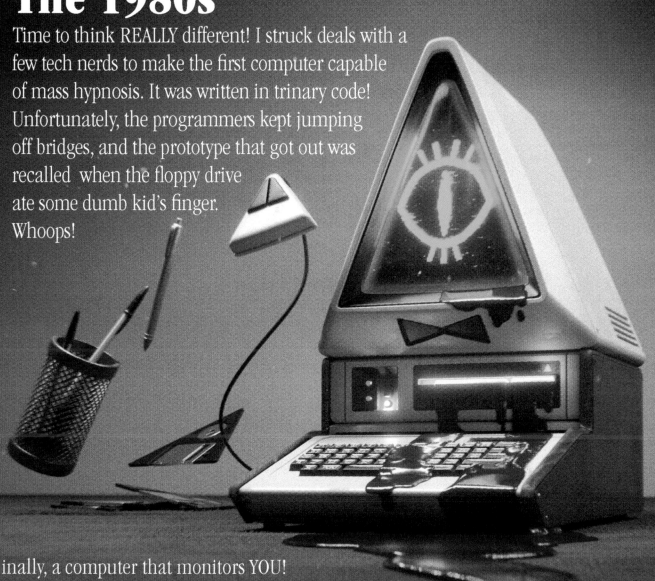

...inally, a computer that monitors YOU!

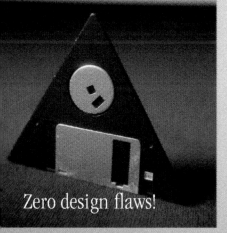

Zero design flaws!

Some of the original Maniacintosh Ciphervision 1000s probably exist in your dad's basement somewhere—see if you can find them! We had two full colors AND a game called "Mind-Sweeper" that deleted your memories! Where's my Game of the Year award, huh??

Maniacintosh™

"*It will eat your finger!!*"

Could these brainwash an army of grandmas into crocheting me a portal? Look, I was running out of ideas, okay! But these were QUALITY products!

THE TRI ANGELS COLLECTION ©

LESS POISON
Now With SLIGHTLY LESS Lead!
MORE VALUE

By Martha

"BEST FWIENDS"

*NOT ACTUAL SIZE

Since 1993, we at **PudgyLilDarlins**™ have been hand-crafting wholesome collectibles, perfect for ages 79–101! Now we're pleased to release the "Tri-Angels" Collection, featuring designs that our founder, Martha Frubbins, hallucinated after accidentally inhaling toxic fumes from cabinet varnish. According to Martha, these adorable little characters represent "my one true master, Cipher be his name, in nightmares may he reign," at which point Martha began to violently shake and foam at the mouth, gibbering in an ancient tongue not known to man. "**ASSEMBLE ALL SEVEN COLLECTIBLES TO OPEN THE SEAL**," she screamed, black ooze leaking from her eyes, as her cats began to levitate. That's our Martha!

CAN *YOU* COLLECT THEM ALL before the end-times come? Bill Cipher, the "King of Fear," will soon be here, riding upon a chariot of chaos, and he will only spare those who bear his collectibles! Don't be left behind!

Bring this advertisement to the store and scream as loud as you can until they give you your very own Tri-Angel!

"SWEET DREAMS"

"GONE FISHIN'!"

Brand New

• *Made with LOVE*

  (Also made from a proprietary carbon, hydrogen, nitrogen, sulphur, and chlorine compound)

• *The perfect weight to kill a man!*

"BLESS OUR TROOPS"

I had to admit it.

My big bet on Earth was starting to look like a bad hand. Every human partner had double-crossed me, gone crazy, or melted from portal radiation. I was toying with the idea of giving up and blowing the horn that summons ⊌ ⤬ ⤬⡇ ⌐ ⌐ to rise from the ocean and drown humanity in brine, when I suddenly felt a shiver through my entire body and started . . . laughing. Uncontrollably. I laughed so hard that the signal was picked up on every radar dish from Antarctica to NASA to the Soviet space station! I laughed so hard every stoplight on Earth turned yellow. I laughed so hard my Henchmaniacs slowly backed out of the room.

SOMEONE HAD DONE IT!

Someone had reversed the Shaman's spell and had summoned me back to Gravity Falls. WHO WOULD IT BE?! A genius? An idiot?

Oh.
Oh my goodness me. YES.

It was both.

Sixer

HIYA, SMART GUY

Gaze upon him, folks! This is what a partner looks like. The ego of a king. The insecurity of a circus freak. And totally isolated from anyone who might steer him clear of my plans. Society calls these people outcasts. I call them Henchmaniacs!

I paid his mind a visit, and OH, what a ROOMY mind it was! This guy's IQ was off the charts— and he was wasting his gifts on, what? Sketching D-list cryptids and collecting moths? (If he ever tries to show you his moth collection, throw yourself off a cliff.)

No, no. I took a little peek through his possible futures and giggled with delight. He was destined for **so much more.** And those hands . . . it was suddenly so clear. The Shaman's zodiac wasn't a cage meant to trap me: it was a TRICK to try to keep me away from the humans I could USE! Me and Sixer would be the perfect team. I had what he always wanted—charisma—and he had what I wanted—fingers.

Since you and me are pals, how's about I give you a peek at something super rare? Sixer was a lot better at science than he was at making friends, and he tended to rip out journal pages that had anything to do with his issues with others . . . especially me. Wanna see what he was hiding? We both know you do.

THE MISSING JOURNAL PAGES

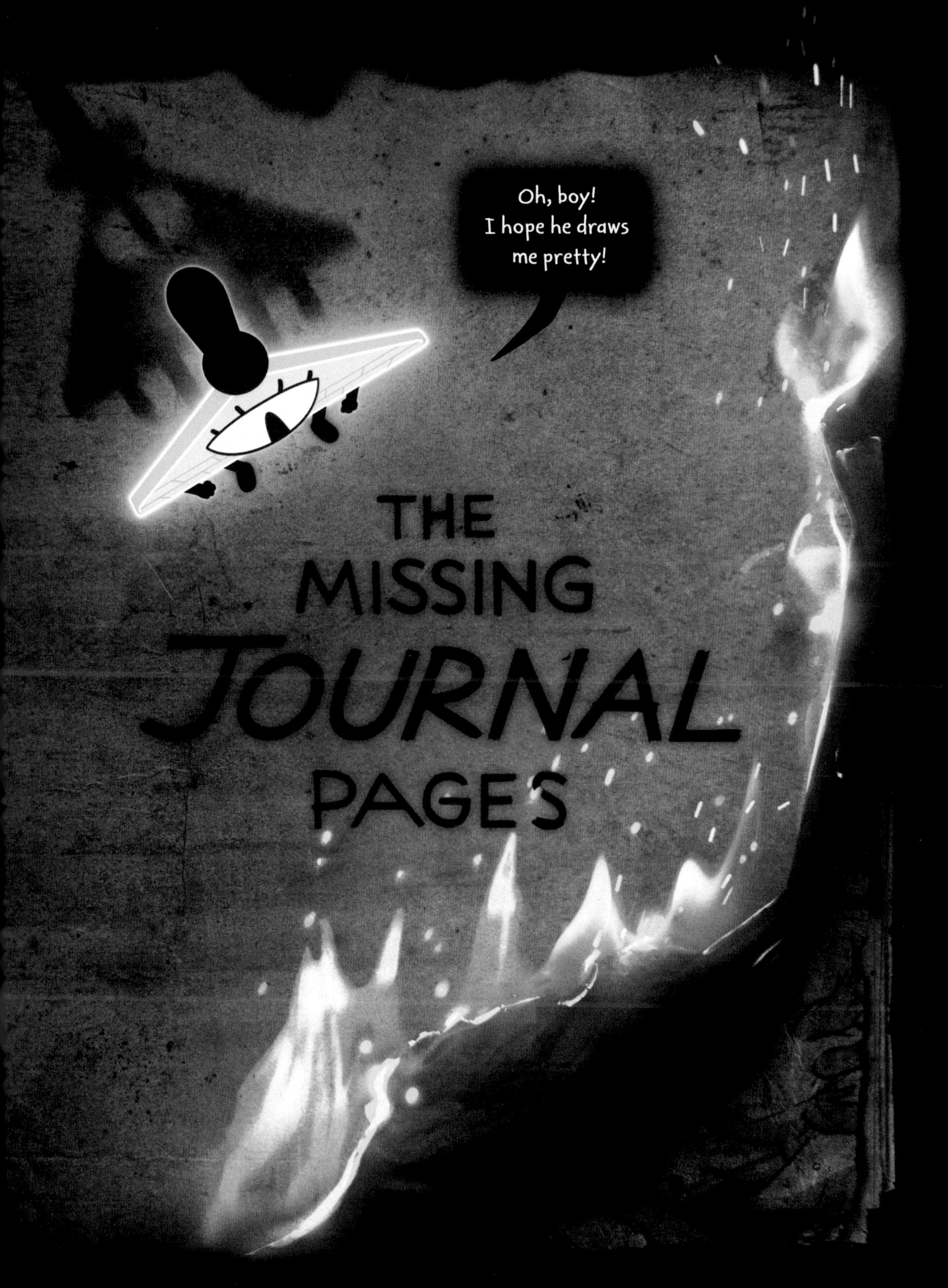

Lost in the Woods

July 3rd— Another day, another failed social interaction. When my waitress told me the apple pie was made "from scratch," I replied, "Incredible! I must meet the chef who created the atoms!" She made a face like she had tasted bleach and ended her shift early. As enamored as I am with this town's marvels, I must confess I have never felt lonelier. The lumberjacks crack jokes at my expense when I try to photograph the Hide Behind, the trick-or-treaters avoid my door on Summerween. (I have so many exciting high-fiber supplements to give out!) A trucker literally shot my chessboard with a shotgun because he said that "tiny horses are the devil's work." Even the local bird watchers banned me after I accidentally set a hawk on fire. (I mistook it for a phoenix! Honest mistake!) Is my strange way of seeing the universe a gift or a curse? Is loneliness just the cost of greatness? And if it is . . . how long am I fated to endure?

CIPHER SPEAKS

Today was the GREATEST. DAY. OF MY LIFE. I keep pacing back and forth trying to make sense of it. I know it sounds crazy, but I've made first contact with an extradimensional deity of knowledge . . . in a top hat. I must consider my actions carefully. I have accidentally stumbled into history. An excerpt of our conversation . . .

"Bill . . . can I call you Bill?"

"YOU CAN CALL ME ANYTHING EXCEPT LATE FOR DINNER! HAHA! THAT'S A JOKE BECAUSE I DON'T HAVE A MOUTH!"

"Are you . . . real? Or just an isolation-induced hallucination? Should I finally do what my college guidance counselor always said and . . . 'seek therapy'?"

"SURE, TAKE LIFE ADVICE FROM A GUY WHO SLEEPS IN HIS OFFICE AT BACKUPSMORE. LIKE MOST TEACHERS, HE WAS JUST INTIMIDATED BY YOUR TALENT AND WAS TRYING TO CURB IT TO FEEL LESS INSECURE ABOUT HIS OWN FAILINGS!"

"My talent?"

"Ding, ding, ding! Guys as smart as you come along once every other century, and they scare the pants off of authority figures! Trust me, I've met 'em all! I see you on the cover of every magazine one day— but only if you make the right chess moves in the game of life, slick! Can I call you slick?"

"You can call me anything except late for dinner."

"Ha! You catch on quick! I think I'm starting to like you, Sixer!"

"I think I'm starting to like you, Bill."

"By the way, that A- you got in 3rd grade? Totally unfair."

"OH my GOD, right??? Thank you!
I maintain it was a—"

"Perfectly legitimate use of an Oxford comma!"

"Perfectly legitimate use of an Oxford comma!"

"Jinx! WOW! Get out of my head!"

"You first."

My Muse & Me

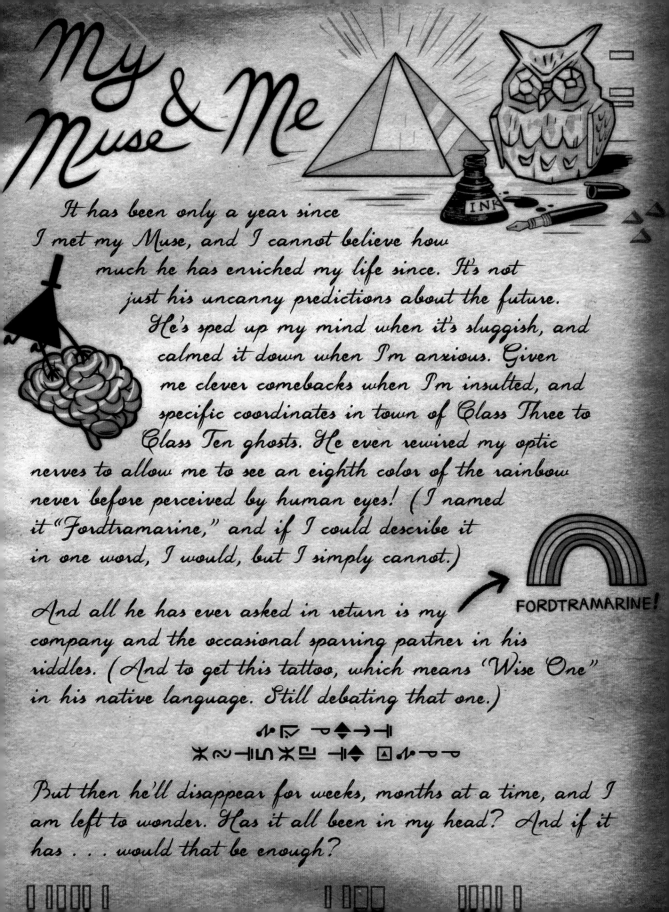

It has been only a year since I met my Muse, and I cannot believe how much he has enriched my life since. It's not just his uncanny predictions about the future. He's sped up my mind when it's sluggish, and calmed it down when I'm anxious. Given me clever comebacks when I'm insulted, and specific coordinates in town of Class Three to Class Ten ghosts. He even rewired my optic nerves to allow me to see an eighth color of the rainbow never before perceived by human eyes! (I named it "Fordtramarine," and if I could describe it in one word, I would, but I simply cannot.)

FORDTRAMARINE!

And all he has ever asked in return is my company and the occasional sparring partner in his riddles. (And to get this tattoo, which means 'Wise One' in his native language. Still debating that one.)

But then he'll disappear for weeks, months at a time, and I am left to wonder. Has it all been in my head? And if it has . . . would that be enough?

June 15th

I was racing around the lab trying to catch a Lockbody Mantis (it had been unlocking doors in my house with it's infernal key arms) when I spotted the calendar. My stomach sank a bit when I realized . . . it was my birthday. This day has felt . . . odd, ever since S and I . . . parted ways. Even worse, I opened my door to find a pile of dead rats inexplicably left there, shaped like the word FORD. I have no idea who would do this. Have I made that many enemies in town already? This seemed as good a sign as any to skip the day and go to bed early.

WHY??

And who should I find waiting for me in my dreams—but my Muse. "Did you like my present? It wasn't easy possessing that many raaaats!" I was dumbfounded . . . he actually remembered my birthday?? I tried to explain that his grasp on human customs was . . . imprecise. "How about I mix you a drink to make it up to you?! It's called the 'Myoclonic Jerk' and it can get you loaded in your sleep. Salvador Dali loved 'em!" I was flattered but politely declined—I'm not much of a drinker. He said, "I'll convince you tomorrow night!" Ha! I doubt it!

I PROBABBLY SHOULDN'T BE WRITIN THIS DOWN
BUT I HAD SUCH A CRAZY??? WOW
WHAT A. IT WAS A NIGHT/ AND NOW
ITS MORNIGN? CILL BIPHER—..
HE DID A DREAM? KARAOKE?
AND THEN ONE THING LED TO
ANOTHER THING AND NORMALLY
I TRY TO SOBER BUT...? HE MIXED
A DREAM DRINK. AND??? GOTTA SAY.
I GOTTA SAY. I JUST GOTTA SAY.
LOOK ITS JUST ME AND MY JOURNAL
HERE, I GOTTA SAY: THIS BILL GUY
ALSO THE RATS WERE HIS IDEA?
I GET IT NOW. I'M GONNA, WERE GONNA
WHAT A TIME. WHAT A HANGOVER.
GONNA WHOLE AD ASPERA ASPERIN
SLEEP. DAY.
—STANFRORD
PI

DISCO GIRL

"GRIFTER"
THE GRIME LIFTER

$150
VALUE!

A SPONGE YOU CAN TRUST!
CALL 1-650-555-GRFT

UNBELIEVABLE!!

A Voice from the Past

I was adjusting my TV antennae for weather reports (looking for ideal conditions for F's first portal test) and spat out my coffee when I saw THIS! My brother hawking scams under the name "Panley Stines." I had half a mind to call that number, just to pretend to be the police, and maybe scare S straight for once! There is something so galling about seeing your OWN FACE committing crimes on your own TV! When my Muse saw me break my stress ball, I decided it was finally time to vent about Stanley.

"How about that; you've got an inferior clone! Why didn't you just eat him in the womb? Think of how powerful you'd be!"

"You can't just eat your twin, Bill."

"You'd be surprised what you can eat! I say sure, call him if you want him to start mooching off you again! Me, I went no contact with my home dimension and I don't regret it. All they did was hold me back and sabotage my talents! Can you imagine?"

"More than you know. But do you ever wonder if maybe . . . maybe things could have been different?"

"Take it from a guy who's tried—you can't undo the past! Unless you want to thaw a giant baby out of a glacier."

"Come again?"

"Figure of speech. It means 'waste your time.'"

"I guess you can never really go home again, can you?"

"I sure can't! My dimension was entirely burned out of existence. Wanna see the only thing left of it?"

Cipher removed his hat, and plucked a single speck of dust from within. The last atoms of a demolished reality. I was dumbfounded.

"What? Your ENTIRE home dimension? destroyed? How? By what?"

Bill looked distant, more distant than I'd ever seen him.

"By a monster."

"That's . . . that's unimaginable. Did you ever track this beast, for revenge? I could help you . . . I could hunt it down!"

He laughed joylessly.

"Sixer, it would eat you alive."

A Winter Break

Winter has come to Gravity Falls! Icicles are hanging from the roof, Christmas specials are playing on TV (<u>Shimmery Twinkleheart Saves Christmas Yet Again 3</u>) and progress on the portal has stalled. A clutch of feral gnomes were hiding from the cold in the dimensional calibrator—it's going to take a week just to unclog the beard hairs!

Unfazed, F has been making hot cocoa and welding rivets while playing Christmas songs on the radio. (These songs make no sense. Why did Rudolph forgive his tormentors for their mockery of his facial deformity? He should have used his red-hot nose to burn his oppressor's workshop to the ground. A lesson to all!)

I'll admit I've never really understood the appeal of the solstice. My father's idea of a Hanukkah present was a "free sample" from the cinder-block factory, and the snow in New Jersey was mostly made of cigar ash and seagull beaks. Our heat budget was so tight that Mom forced S and me to wear one sweater at the same time. (She called it the "Abominable Snow-Stan." Our cat lived in fear of it year-round.)

← LOCAL
ENGLISH HOLLY

LAB SNOW GLOBE

Lost in work, I was taken by surprise today when J presented me with a gift: a **SNOW GLOBE** he'd built of our lab, complete with glitter snow. I had to laugh at the the notion of our secret hidden fortress having "merchandise." And even more thoughtful—he'd knitted me a pair of six-fingered gloves! (You have no idea how hard those are to find in stores.)

SIX FINGERED
GLOVES

But my delight quickly soured to shame—it hadn't occurred to me to get him anything at all. J reassured me that being part of scientific history was present enough. He only wished to hold my Nobel Prize one day. This was more than I could bear—I told him we were taking the weekend off. Maybe we could hunt a yeti for holiday sweater fur. Why, I might even go so far as to purchase some sort of "nog."

But J confessed that he's flying back home to visit Emma-May this week, leaving me in the lab alone for the holiday. Of course . . . who could fault him? I sometimes forget there is a world outside my lab.

I hope my Muse visits soon . . .
He's been strangely absent for weeks. . . .

Isolation was taking its toll when I heard a loud BANG
and voices outside my door. Had I returned after all?
Had he brought his family? Alas, I went out and
found my porch deserted, and stranger still . . .

MYSTERY FOOTPRINTS

THEY DISAPPEAR!

They start and stop in . . . the center of the snow. How
could this be? Neither ghosts nor Boy Scouts leave without
properly harassing the homeowner, and the smell of smoke
in the air suggested an otherworldly
event.

CHILD SIZED

Either way, if there were children lost
on my property, they'd need to be found
at once. I grabbed my lantern and
headed out to investigate. Over the years I've become an
expert in identifying tracks in Gravity Falls, and I wasn't
about to let these go unidentified . . .

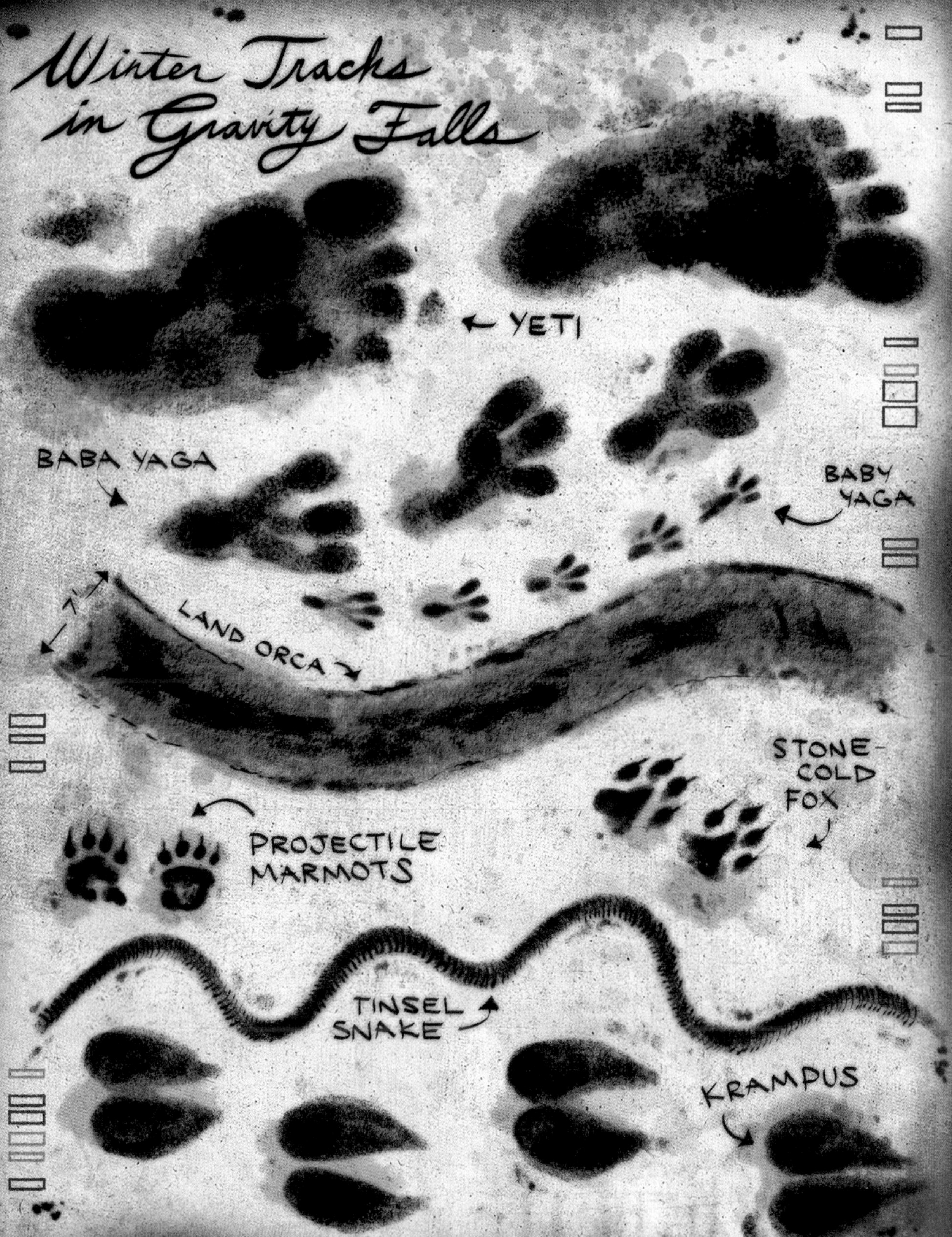

Winter Tracks in Gravity Falls

← YETI

BABA YAGA

BABY YAGA

LAND ORCA →

PROJECTILE MARMOTS

STONE-COLD FOX

TINSEL SNAKE

KRAMPUS

Snowed In

DRAT! Within minutes I fell victim to Gravity Falls's unpredictable weather. (We go from Paleozoic blizzards to freak heat waves to "quail hail" multiple times per winter.) With the cold snap snapping after me, I hid in a cavern to stave off frostbite. But that's when I noticed something even more chilling than the weather. There was a second set of footprints behind me. Cloven. I heard jingling in the air, the whooshing of branches, and then—

DARKNESS. When I came to, I found myself tied up in a massive barrel, delirious, being carried through the snow. I turned to see I wasn't alone; four frightened children were with me. I knew immediately what I was dealing with. I sighed for being so stupid.

The Krampus
Scourge of the solstice!
"NAUGHTY KIDS" BARREL
CINNAMON BREATH
LISTEN FOR JINGLING!

The Krampus began to speak. My Folk German is rusty, but it translated to something along the lines of "Ahh, mein little naughty boys und girls have awakened! Please, stuff your mouths with mein plum delights for all!" I addressed the barreled children.

"Kids, I'm going to tell it straight. No fairy tale that starts with free candy ever ends well for children. Especially German ones. Sorry, Hans. Follow my exact instructions if you want to live." They nodded their pink faces as I sighed and asked what supernatural price he demanded for our freedom. He was clearly expecting this question.

"I will only release you if you tell me one piece of holiday cheer you brought another." That did it. My tolerance for his fairy-tale nonsense had reached rock bottom. "God, folklore cryptids are always so moralistic. Literally, who are you to say how I should live my damn life? How are YOU judging me?! You're a naked goat vagrant who puts babies in barrels! You're lucky I don't have any grenades on me!"

With his claw, he drew a glowing red pentagram in the snow, and I could see the ground begin to open up to his lair.

On the bright side, it seemed very warm! On the downside, it looked like hell. My Muse was nowhere to be found. I was just wondering what my obituary would look like when—CLANG. The KRAMPUS was out cold with a concussion. A powerful figure appeared, backlit by the sun, holding . . . a banjo? It was . . . my assistant! F!

We embraced. I couldn't believe he was back so soon! He explained that his family reunion had been less than ideal. It seems he and his wife got in a massive fight when she realized he'd forgotten to get her . . . a Christmas present.

I asked if there was anything that could cheer him up. Maybe we could kick the passed-out Krampus? The children were all beating it with sticks and having a great time! But F was devastated and trembling from the encounter. The holiday hadn't turned out how he hoped, and he had no cheer left. He retreated to his quarters, defeated . . .

That night, I called F into the lab for an urgent portal update! I'll admit that it wasn't the most efficient use of our electricity, but the smile on his face proved I'd made the right choice. I even put on his favorite song, "Grandma Got Run Over by a Reindeer" (a sacrifice graver than any I have ever known).

He asked if I was finally coming around on holidays, or if this was just to keep the Krampus from coming back. I told him it was time to drink nog until we couldn't remember what a Krampus was. We spent the rest of the night building snowmen and reminiscing about old times. It can be hard sometimes to find a moment to celebrate when you're lost in the cold . . . but it's easier with new gloves.

The Muse Returns

The next morning, I awoke from my nog-coma to find my Muse perched on my shelf like a watchful elf.

"Happy Halloween! Catch any leprechauns?"

I was so startled I dropped J's snow globe, which shattered on the ground. I couldn't hide my frustration any longer. After all this time, he chose to show up now? I was almost roasted by a Krampus, and where was he? Off inspiring some other scientist? Posing for some tapestry? Were we even partners? He threw the accusation back in my face.

"Hey, I'm not the one skipping portal work to carouse with a third-wheel hillbilly with second thoughts about our project!"

I started to argue—but he had a point. J has seemed less and less committed to work lately.

"I have it on good authority that he daydreams about shutting the whole thing down. I'm just saying . . . keep an eye on him."

I was embarrassed by my outburst. The isolation had made me paranoid. I apologized for my lapse in composure. My Muse brushed it off.

"Don't sweat it, pal! When in doubt, I've got a simple trick I use to figure out who to believe."

"What's that?" I eagerly inquired.

"Trust No One."

STANLEY PINES

"I can fit my whole fist in my mouth."

College:

Who's Asking?

Social Clubs:

Stanley Pines Fan Club! (only member)

Senior Standout:

Least likely to escape New Jersey

Academic Rank:

(In lieu of an answer, Stanley submitted a drawing of a possum with a knife.)

NERD

STANFORD PINES

"Ad Astra Per Aspera"

College:

West Coast Tech BACKUPSMORE

Social Clubs:

Chess Club, Honors Society, Robotics Team, Metric System Advocacy Society, Mathletes, Grammarkateers, Astrono-Masters, Pedants Association (Actually we prefer "Association of Pedants," please issue this correction or prepare to receive a very lengthy series of letters)

Senior Standout:

Most likely to succeed

Academic Rank:

Valedictorian

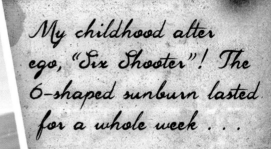

My childhood alter ego, "Six Shooter"! The 6-shaped sunburn lasted for a whole week . . .

DAMN! This morning I found F rummaging through my old copy of <u>Urban Legends of New Jersey</u>, where I had forgotten I had hidden some old personal items! I've quickly re-hidden them here, away from prying eyes. Perhaps my Muse is right that F is getting too close . . .

Dream, or Warning?

My heart pounds in my chest and the hairs stand on my neck as I write this entry. I've awoken from a dream like none I've experienced. It was a crisp, clear day, and I was sketching a yellow meadowlark in a birch clearing, whistling some 1960s radio tune I'd forgotten the words to (James and Bobby, I believe?) when the bird flew off, startled. From the darkness of the forest, a horde of lost souls from throughout history lurched toward me, black liquid oozing from their mouths. Their limbs hung limply, as if from strings, and they began to speak in unison, repeating the same words over and over, like a skipping record:

"I GROW MADDENED"

I desperately tried to ask them what they meant, but no matter how hard I screamed, no sound came out. As the chanting grew louder, the forest was suddenly ENGULFED in flames, screaming laughter echoing, and then—I awoke on the floor, gasping for breath, having tumbled from my bed.

WHAT DOES IT MEAN?

I feel strongly that this was a warning, but of what? The more I thought about it, the more I "grew maddened" myself. But then I remembered my childhood love of ANAGRAMS. (When I rearranged the letters in local bully Brad Hodgel's name to spell "Hog Bladder," he never made fun of me again!) I grabbed the magnetic letters on my fridge and got to work decoding. But with every try, my frustration only increased!

POSSIBLE ANAGRAMS

------ --------- I GROW MADDENED

A   DREADED MOWING
WEDGED   DREAMED GOD WIN
NIMROD   WARNED DEMIGOD
DEMON WAR DID EDGE
IM DEAD WRONGED
DEGRADE MIND...OW!

Drat. The answer eludes me. The weather has cleared again, and conditions are nearly perfect for the big day. J has invited me to dinner at Greasy's tonight to toast tomorrow's test. Maybe my mind will clear too after the triumph of our launch . . .

I WAS WRONG ABOUT EVERYTHING!

I'VE SHUT DOWN THE PORTAL!
DAMN IT ALL!

My mind reels from horror and humiliation. How could I have been so foolish as to let Bill into my mind, and how can I prevent his coming apocalypse?! F has abandoned me for my hubris, and Cipher has gone suspiciously silent. There's no time to lose— I must DESTROY THE PORTAL, BURN MY JOURNALS, AND LEAVE TOWN FOREVER! I'm setting out to get firewood now. Torment me all you want, Cipher, but your games are finally over.

3:00 AM

I have stared at the fire, journals in hand, for hours. I just can't do it. The knowledge in here could be a gift to mankind, the portal's potential limitless. Am I really going to destroy it all just out of spite? No, I won't give HIM the satisfaction! Instead of destroying my work, I'll find a way to DESTROY BILL INSTEAD. If Cipher has a weakness, I'll find it. I'll outsmart the devil yet!

He may be a god, but I am a scientist.

Step One: Finding a way to prevent Cipher from entering my lab and restarting the portal while I'm asleep. The door is password protected, but Cipher can enter my mind, so he'll know everything I know—codes, hidden keys, and all. HOW CAN I KEEP CIPHER OUT BUT LET MYSELF IN?

9:00 AM

IT WORKED! Last night I installed a RETINAL SCANNER. Bill's possession subtly alters the shape of his victims' pupils. Now I can get into my lab while awake but Bill cannot! However, that didn't stop him from trying . . .

This morning I awoke to find my knuckles bloody and sore. Cipher must have been punching and scraping the steel door like a caged animal all night in a frenzy to get in. Break my bones if you must, Cipher, but you cannot break my will! I will research a way to eradicate your tether to my world, keep my journals, and earn my renown yet! I'm off to the library to see if I can find some weakness that may lead to Cipher's downfall!

ꓷꙄꛎꝋꝒꙄꙄꓷꝒꝒꙄꝅ Ꝓꝧ ꝒꝋꙄꝒꙄꝋꝒꙄꝒ ꙄꝒꝒꝋ ꝧꙄꝒꝧ ꝒꝧꙄꝋ
ꝒꙄꝒꝧꝋꙄꙄꝒ ꝧꙄꝧ Ꙅꝋꝓꝧꝋ ꝋꝓ ꝋꝓ ꝧꙄꝒꙄꝋ...

The Bad News: I've been banned from the library. The children were complaining about my smell. You're smelling science, children! The good news: I've discovered lost archives of a FORGOTTEN BILL-HUNTING SOCIETY! *Though their methods are laughably out-of-date, some of their ideas are worth building on. Behold my new and improved:*

BILL-PROOF SUIT

I. ANTI-SLEEP MEASURES
Headphones will play a loop of common grammar mistakes. There's no way I'll sleep through that!

2. DECOY BRAIN
To capture Cipher! When he tries to escape, the synaptic twitching will activate the trigger on the . . .

3. DUAL FLAMETHROWER
Incinerating the false brain and, hopefully, Bill inside.

4. DEFIBRILLATOR
Possession will trigger a thousand-volt shock, jolting Bill out of my body. (Rubber boots should mitigate personal injury.)

5. SPELLS & SILVER BULLETS
My brother once mocked me when I slept with a wooden stake under my pillow because our neighbor was suspiciously pale. Turned out our neighbor was just Scandinavian, but better safe than sorry. Every magical weapon and incantation referenced in Journal 2 will be at the ready!

6. BILL-DETECTING VISOR
I've tried using a small light to detect possession, but these will be infinitely superior.

7. CLOAK SEWN FROM UNICORN HAIR
Will need to convince a unicorn that I'm pure of heart. (May need to invent heart-purification ray for this part.)

ZOM-BILLS!

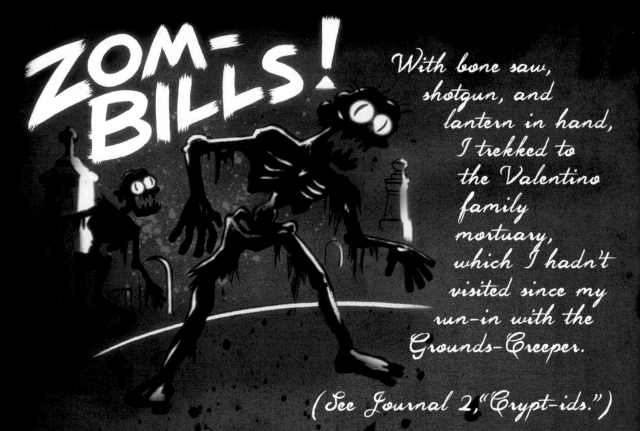

With bone saw, shotgun, and lantern in hand, I trekked to the Valentino family mortuary, which I hadn't visited since my run-in with the Grounds-Creeper.

(See Journal 2, "Crypt-ids.")

I reminded myself as I crowbarred my way into the morgue that 19th-century doctors frequently robbed graves in the name of science! Surely this was morally justified and wouldn't incur any sort of "curse." No sooner had I retrieved a brain than I noticed the ground start to shake beneath me. It was at this moment that I learned two interesting facts:

1) BILL CIPHER CAN POSSESS CORPSES?
2) BILL CIPHER CAN POSSESS CORPSES!

From the GRAVES AROUND ME arose a HORDE of CACKLING CADAVERS, EYES AGLOW. I raced for the car, blasting the invaders with my shotgun until only one stood, blocking my way. Shotgun in hand, I demanded answers.

"Why are you doing this?! Why won't you just leave me alone?" Even without a tongue, the zombie spoke in Cipher's unmistakable voice.

"Oh, come on, Sixer. We both know you don't really want to be left alone. Admit it, you LOVE how important I make you feel. And I love having a pet human in my pocket. It's a win-win!"

"Don't forget which one of us is holding a gun!" I warned him. He grinned an inhumanly wide grin.

"Fordsy, nobody else really gets you, do they? Without me, you'll always feel unseen, surrounded by dolts who don't recognize your true potential. You've always felt alone in a crowd, haven't you? Who else will give you this feeling again? Even if you got rid of me, you'd miss me. Admit it, you'd miss me."

13 GAUGE

AMMO!

I hesitated. "I have missed you," I replied. He smiled.

"But my aim is getting better."

I BLASTED the last Zom-Bill to the ground, then shot two more times and spat where I stood. I was so exhausted I could barely stand. But I knew falling asleep would make ME his next zombie. I picked up the brain and made my way home as snow began to fall. I'll admit I was pretty proud of my comeback . . . Pretty sure I heard that from Dad . . .

9:00 AM

Frustration mounts. Without F's mechanical skill, constructing the suit seems impossible. Worse still, every time I doze off, I awaken to find these . . . stuck to my forehead. I keep replying with notes of my own, only to wake up to more. This is getting out of hand.

CAN WE TALK?
NO!
PRETTY PLEASE?
I'D RATHER DIE!
OH, DON'T BE SO DRAMATIC
I'M AN AUTHOR, WE'RE ALL DRAMATIC.
HEY WANNA HEAR A JOKE?
NO
KNOCK KNOCK!
NOT NOW! I HAVE A HEADACHE
THAT'S BECAUSE I'VE BEEN KNOCK-KNOCKING YOUR SKULL AGAINST THE WALL!
HA HA HA HA HA HA HA HA HA HA HA HA HA HA HA
STOP WASTING MY POST-IT NOTES!

VENOM STAIN

WAKEY WAKEY!

HERE'S A SNAKEY!

DAMN! I awoke this morning to find a western diddleback rattlesnake taped into my journal! I managed to contain it in a terrarium without getting bitten. (I think.) But my patience is reaching its limit!

VERY WELL, CIPHER!

IF IT'S WAR YOU WANT, IT'S WAR YOU'LL GET!

IF YOU WANT TO TORTURE ME?
I'LL TORTURE YOU BACK!

The World Is Small
Ever After for Always

SIDE A

0 50 0

INKWELL

SEE THIS CASSETTE?

I KNOW YOU RECOGNIZE IT!

THAT'S RIGHT, YOUR FAVORITE SONG!

I'M GOING TO LISTEN TO THIS ON LOOP
UNTIL IT'S STUCK IN MY HEAD,
WHICH WILL MEAN IT'S STUCK IN YOURS!

I WONDER WHAT AN EARWORM FEELS LIKE
WHEN YOU LIVE FOR ETERNITY? READY TO FIND OUT??

WHAT DO YOU HAVE TO SAY TO THAT?!

The War in my Mind

??? AM

A horrifying morning. A blast of cold air jolted me awake to find myself not lying in bed, but standing upright on the roof with icicles stuck to my face, shivering, nearly blue from hypothermia, peering down at the ground far below. Bill brought me here. I know he could have made me jump. But he didn't. Why? To send a message: that I'm his toy. He could spare me or take my life away. If I'm still alive, it's because he wants to make a deal. I saw smoke coming from the chimney and heard music thumping from inside. Could Bill have burned my journals in my sleep?! I raced to my living room only to find a cup of tea and a chess set laid out on the coffee table, an 8-track of "Sweet Dreams" by the Eurythmics playing, a fire lit in the fireplace, and the fridge magnets arranged into a message.

LOOKY HERE

PLAY ME

I put the tape in the VCR and was stunned. I almost didn't recognize the wild-eyed hermit staring back on the TV: it was me. Or rather, Bill in my body, from the previous night. He'd recorded a message.

"WELCOME BACK TO PUPPET HOUR WITH BILL! SAY HI, KIDS! TODAY'S PUPPET IS MY OLD PAL SIXER. SIXER'S HAD A ROUGH DAY. BUT HIS NIGHT WAS EVEN ROUGHER. WANNA SEE?"

Cipher proceeded to play a horrifying montage he had filmed the night before of himself taking a joyride IN MY BODY! Every time the camera cut, it would jump to some increasingly mortifying scene. As though that weren't enough, he left Polaroids of my night scattered across my floor like a mental patient's scrapbook!

"PARTYING"

MUST BURN
THIS PHOTO

MUST REMOVE
WITH LASERS

MY WHOLE
BODY HURTS

WHY WOULD HE DO THIS?

Rabble-rousing! Unsafe working conditions! A tattoo that I would never agree to under any circumstances! Blemishes to my spotless criminal record!

DISRESPECTING THE LAW

I KEEP COUGHING UP SPIDERS

Has he done this before?? How FAR would he go?!

But then he crossed a line. Helplessly I watched Cipher in my own body limp up to a pay phone and dial . . . STANLEY'S phone number from the infomercial?! No. He wouldn't.

"Hey, brother, it's Sixer. I'm going to take a swim in the frozen lake tomorrow, and I might not ever come back, so if you don't hear from me, I just want you to know that it's because I never loved you. BUH-BYEEEEE."

My heart was in my throat until I heard the dial tone . . . The pay phone was out of order. The message hadn't gotten through. Cipher turned back to address me.

"TSK, TSK, TSK. LOOK WHAT YOU MADE ME MAKE YOU DO! TOMORROW'S TAPE IS GONNA BE MUCH WORSE. WANT THE SHOW TO END? GO DOWNSTAIRS AND TURN ON THE PORTAL. OR I'M GONNA HAVE TO SHOW YOU WHAT I'M REALLY CAPABLE OF."

I was livid. I hurled the tape into the fire and screamed, "You have NO POWER HERE! You're just in my MIND! I can outlast anything you can—" when . . . suddenly . . . something started to feel . . . off . . . My vision flickered.

The clock had stopped ticking.

SOMETHING WAS WRONG . . . THEN BLACKNESS BLACKNESS BLACKNESS BLACKNESS BLACKNESS

Where was I? My body was paralyzed. I felt my bones being pulled slowly, slowly out of their sockets. It was excruciating. I tried to scream, but nothing came out . . .

"THINK, SIXER. YOU LET ME. IN. YOUR. HEAD. DO YOU REALIZE WHAT I CAN DO IN HERE IF I WANT? I CAN FLIP A SWITCH THAT MAKES EVERY NEURON BURN WITH PAIN BEYOND IMAGINATION. I CAN REWIRE YOUR OPTIC NERVE SO THE SKY IS BELOW YOU, PLAY A TONE THAT GETS LOUDER AND LOUDER UNTIL YOU BASH IN YOUR OWN SKULL JUST TO MAKE IT STOP. I CAN DELETE MEMORIES RANDOMLY, JUST FOR FUN. MAYBE I ALREADY HAVE. WHAT DO YOU WANT TO REMEMBER. YOUR MOTHER'S FACE? YOUR OWN NAME? WHO ARE YOU ANYWAY?"

"That's ridiculous!" I shouted. "I'm . . . I'm . . ." I panicked. I couldn't recall my name. I began to shake.

He flipped his finger like he was turning on a light switch, and it came to me.

"I'm Stanf—"

Flipped again. I went blank. I felt my sockets start to strain. Any second my tendons would pop, my bones would splinter. I fell to the ground, on the verge of vomiting.

"YOU'RE MY PROPERTY. DON'T FORGET IT. The hillbilly abandoned you, your father won't want you returning without millions, you have no friends, and if you died out here in the snow, who would even miss you? Turn on the portal. I'VE WAITED TOO LONG FOR THIS. BY THE WAY, I'M SENDING SOMEONE TO STEAL YOUR EYES. THAT'S NOT A JOKE. I HAVE A FRIEND THAT WILL STEAL. YOUR EYES. You have 72 hours. DON'T CROSS ME AGAIN."

I awoke from the hallucination, heart pounding, to find myself back in my living room, clock ticking, record skipping—and
began to weep. He's right. What was I thinking?! Throughout all recorded history, none have stopped Bill. Who was I
to believe I could be the first? Only one man in the world
could possibly help me. I ransacked F's notes for any hint of his
whereabouts, but only found two remaining items in his desk:
5 failed prototypes for the perfect 6-fingered gloves . . . and this
ripped photo from the day in college when we became roommates.
There was nothing else. He was gone.

I'm out of options. The caves. The same symbols that summoned
Cipher must hold the key to stopping him. The snow has begun to
fall again and there's very little time. There's only one left I can
turn to to protect my journals while I prepare for the journey . . .

Should I Contact S?

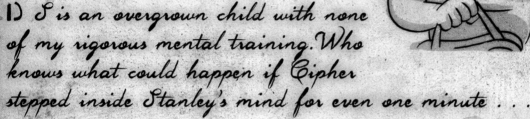

CONS:

1) S is an overgrown child with none of my rigorous mental training. Who knows what could happen if Cipher stepped inside Stanley's mind for even one minute . . .

2) What if Stanley somehow manages to destroy the portal just like he destroyed my perpetual motion machine? I suppose that machine did work in its own way . . . It kept me perpetually angry for years. ⬤X%$⚡☺$$☠♨?? ⬤X&♯⬤ X** X*?☺☂?

3) What if he tries to rope me into his latest get-rich-quick scheme? His latest commercial was for "Stan Sauce: The Miracle Sauce that's too cool for the FDA!"

4) What if . . . he mocks me? What if he sees that I abandoned our family to become a recluse on the brink of madness? Could I risk admitting that I was . . . wrong?

PROS:

I have no one else.

Well, that settles it. It's time to come face-to-face with a face I haven't seen in 10 years. My own face. Which . . . is my brother's face. God, I miss sleep.

I GROW MADDE...

LOSING SIXER

Oh, the melodrama. Do you really buy that sob story? "MY POOR BRAIN!" "MY POOR KNUCKLES!" **Please!** I was never REALLY going to "steal his eyes." Those were just practical jokes! Some light hazing to initiate him into my gang, just like the rest of my Henchmaniacs! It's not my fault if Mr. Tabletop Gaming rolled a zero on sense of humor! But after this one little spat, Fordsy swore "eternal vengeance," shut down the portal, and dedicated himself to "hunting me down throughout the multiverse." Obsessed much? I know Sixer secretly loved our "will-they-won't-they-destroy-the-world" relationship. This was just his way of keeping things spicy! But the gang was worried. What about our crumbling Nightmare Realm? I told them to relax, I had it all figured out. So we had a minor setback? Big deal! I knew Ford would be back!

I wasn't upset at all! In fact, I decided to prove how not upset I was about our falling-out by knocking back a few cold glasses of "I'm Fine Juice" at O'Sadley's Multidimensional Pub in the Rock Bottom Asteroid Belt of the Vicious Spiral Nebula! The rest of that night gets a little hazy, but according to the police transcripts apparently things took a turn . . .

DIMENSIONAL AUTHORITY
CALL TRANSCRIPT

EVIDENCE

1	**POLICE:**	Dimensional Authority. What's your emergency?
2		
3	**WOMAN:**	Hi, yeah, I'm working the drive-through window at Burrito
4		Paradox Interdi-Mexican Restaurant, and there's a—
5		[muffled sounds of explosions and screaming in the
6		background] There's a triangle, I think he's had a lot to
7		drink, he ordered "one Sixer, please." We told him that
8		didn't make any sense, and he started crying, and then
9		ordered "infinite empanadas," and we told him we don't
10		offer infinite empanadas anymore after they caused all
11		those time loops, and then he started just, like, trashing
12		the place. He's inside the milkshake machine right now
13		spinning and—[incomprehensible]
14		
15	**POLICE:**	Is anyone hurt, ma'am?
16		
17	**WOMAN:**	Our manager, like, his body glitched through the ceiling
18		and his legs keep kicking and it's making the light fixtures
19		swing around. There's a kid who is crying super loud
20		because his head was turned into a CGI watermelon. Okay,
21		the triangle just filled the Mountain Dew machine with
22		blood and he just glued two customers together? There's
23		nothing in the employee handbook about how to handl
24		
25	**POLICE:**	Stay calm, ma'am, we're dispatching officers right now to
26		
27	**WOMAN:**	Hey, hey, he's grabbing the phone away from me, I can't—
28		
29	**BILL CIPHER:**	Hi, MOM, this is BILLY. I want you to [incomprehensible].
30		I'm gonna be back from school soon—don't forget to cut the
31		crust off my SANDWICHES or I'll [incomprehensible].
32		Where did you all go? WHERE DID [sound of approaching
33		police sirens] YOU HEAR THAT? My MARIACHI BAND is
		RIGHT ON TIME—
		END OF CALL

BURRITO PARADOX™

THINK OUTSIDE KNOWN LOGIC

A MINOR SETBACK

I don't care for captivity. Even though I only spent six hours in Dimensional Authority Lockup for "indecent exposure" before Keyhole picked the lock and 8 Ball ate the guards, those six hours felt like an eternity. I vowed right then and there—no more playing nice with the humans. I should never have given Sixer three days to comply with my orders! What was I, a saint? And why did I do it—some misplaced sentimentality? Never again! If I got another chance to get that portal open, I wasn't going to miss it. And I got my second chance, all right!

WEIRDMAGEDDON

Look, you already know what happened next! Using tenth-dimensional cunning and charisma, I returned to Gravity Falls, played the family against each other, and FINALLY got the BRIDGE BETWEEN WORLDS that I'd dreamed of for so long! And that stupid prophecy didn't stop me! In your face, Shaman! Do we really need to dwell on what happened afterward?

Yes, I was shattered. YES, it was a dirty trick. NO, I'm not upset. Because since then, I've gained the ability to finally find a human partner better than Ford in every way. After infinite disappointments, infinite failures, I've found a human partner who won't double-cross me or jerk me around! One who UNDERSTANDS the TRAGEDY of my GREAT VISION DENIED!

I'VE FOUND YOU!

I think it's finally time to tell you . . . my plans.

THE PLAN

I've got a confession to make, amigo! This whole time, while you've been consuming my book's riveting "content" like a piglet suckling wisdom-milk, I've been inside your brain making some . . . changes. Only little things! Snipping out your SHAME and FEAR CENTERS, deleting useless memories (who needs to remember the year 2017?) and hyperdeveloping your Hypnagogic Lobe to make you the perfect conduit for . . . my plans. Why do you think I actually wanted all that blood? For "INK"? Get wise, kid! I needed it to induce mild delirium so you wouldn't notice my tune-ups! Just standard sleight of hand, I assure you—all for the greater good! Focus on the doughnut, not the hole, Jack! Because you're about to become the MOST IMPORTANT PERSON IN HISTORY!

THE VESSEL

Your mind is finally tuned just right for the big day. You get to go to Gravity Falls, shake my statue's hand, and then IT HAPPENS. WE TRADE PLACES I take over your body, and you get to hang out in my cushy VIP pad in the afterlife while I use your meatmobile to fire up one of the earth's remaining portals. Once I restart Weirdmageddon, we'll swap back and RULE THE WORLD TOGETHER!

THERE'S NO WAY IT CAN GO WRONG!!

I've never done this from beyond the grave, so there's a chance it could kill us both, but NO RISK, NO REWARD. I removed your hesitance neurons and amped up your impulsivity center, so I KNOW you want to do it! A free vacation from your body, and when you wake up, WORLD DOMINATION!

YOUR MISSION

I. GO TO GRAVITY FALLS, SHAKE MY HAND.

II. I USE YOUR BODY TO BOOT UP A PORTAL! MAYBE THAT DARK AGES ONE STILL WORKS!

III. WITH MY POWERS RETURNED, I REASSEMBLE MY SCATTERED ATOMS FROM ACROSS REALITY TO LIVE AGAIN! WE BOTH GET OUR BODIES BACK!

IV. WEIRDMAGEDDON 2.0, BABY! WE TURN THE SKY PLAID, CRUSH THE PRESIDENT INTO A FINE PASTE, AND RULE LIKE GODS! (MAY FLOOD EVERY CITY, SET OFF THE VOLCANOES, SPLIT THE EARTH IN HALF, BLAH BLAH BLAH.)

V. I KILL THE PINES. WITH SHARP OBJECTS! BYEEEEEEEEEEEEEEEEEE!

VI. FIESTA TIME! I'VE ALREADY BOUGHT A PIÑATA! IT WILL BE FILLED WITH THE PINES' ORGANS!

POSSIBLE DEATH TOLL:	POSSIBLE FUN TOLL:
7.8 BILLION	INFINITE!

You wanted your life to have meaning—this is it! You're in it with me, ride or die, for the ULTIMATE PRIZE! EVERYONE WILL FEAR YOU! YOU'LL EVEN FEAR YOURSELF! AND UNLIKE THAT BACKSTABBER SIXER, YOU WON'T BACK DOWN WHEN THE KITCHEN GETS HOT! Right? RIGHT???

I ONLY HAVE ONE QUESTION:

ARE YOU WITH ME?

Yes, it's me again. No, I'm not going to give you another lecture. I realize I cannot admonish you for reading along any more than I can admonish myself for the same sin. It's true, I've hesitated in throwing this book away. I found myself drawn into a familiar whirlpool of what-ifs. What if this book contained secrets needed to protect my family? What if throwing it in the rift is what Bill wanted all along? Was he using double reverse psychology? Or is that what he wanted me to think?

I emerged from my lab after days of agonized contemplation to find—to my shock—that Mabel was reading the book, out loud, to Stanley, Dipper, Soos, and Wendy! I tried to explain the terrible danger that they were in, when I realized: None of them were possessed. None of them were harmed. And they had tears in their eyes... from laughing at his attempts to deceive them!

It hit me all at once. The real reason I had kept the book secret. I thought I was protecting my family, but I was really protecting myself . . . from humiliation.

Shame is a powerful emotion. But it grows in the dark. The more I've tried to hide my past with Bill, the more hold it's had over me!

But sharing it with them, it went from a dark secret . . . to a joke. They didn't see me as an irredeemable screwup. Stanley said, "So, your past is just a giant pile of mistakes? Congratulations—you really are a Pines!" And as we read the book together, it became increasingly clear. This isn't some dark bible or cursed gateway—it's the last pathetic gasp of a has-been who fears being forgotten. Bill isn't a god, he's a needy theater kid in search of a stage.

He's making it all up as he goes along. All he really wants is for us to keep reading. Because as long as <u>we're</u> reading, we're giving him his real lifeblood: not power, <u>attention</u>. You can't kill an idea, but you can think of a better one. Bill may tell you that happiness requires conquering galaxies and living forever, but I've seen enough of the universe to tell you that he's wrong. I've found my happiness. And it looks like this:

Speaking of which . . . there's someone who's been wanting to say hello . . .

Hiii!!!!! Mabel here! I just got a new pen that's, like . . . five pens in one? So I'm gonna write each sentence in a different color and it'll be like reading a rainbow!

Okay, so Grunkle Ford asked for me to write a warning in this **evil book**! When I looked inside, it said "A Guide to Everyone Who Ever Had a Crush on You." But then it asked for my blood?? Nice try, buster! This gal only gives her blood to hot vampire doctors!

Anyway, Bill seems to me like a super-needy ex, and I think we can all agree—time to move on, girl! Bill, if you're reading this from space or hell or wherever, here's my tips for getting over Grunkle Ford!

1) Try dyeing or cutting your hair! Nothing says "moving on" like breakup bangs! Wait, do you even have hair? Get hair! Then do something different with it!

2) Rebound! Go crush on someone else's uncle! Actually, maybe stay away from uncles for a while. Work on you!

3) Talk it out! I tell all my problems to my thera-pig, Dr. Waddles, MD. ("MD" stands for "My Darling.")

Anyway Bill—you tried to kill my brother. If I ever see you again I'm doing this!

Deal with it!

MABEL PINES

This is Dipper Pines, mystery hunter, survivor of the apocalypse, scribe of the dark unknown

AND FUTURE RUNWAY SHORTS MODEL!

Mabel! You had your own page! Anyway, to the reader— your obsession with Bill? I get it, man! But sometimes hunting monsters can turn you into a monster yourself. Don't forget to also hunt down sunshine, friends, and the occasional shower.

Bill, if you're somehow reading this from whatever quantum afterlife you wormed your way into, listen up, man. You tried to kill my sister. If I ever see you again outside of my nightmares, there is no force in the universe that will stop me from putting you in the ground. I outsmarted the US government, leapt off a cliff and punched through a robot's head, defeated zombies, outsleuthed Sherlock Holmes, and survived the start of puberty. Come at us again and I'll end you.

Wow, Dipper!! So confident!!

Was it . . . was it too confident?

No, it was just right! 13 looks good on you!

Technically a teen,

DIPPER PINES

PS: △ ⊔Ӡ┱ ◇⊹⑁△⁑⋀ ⊔⍋⋔⋀▽ ⸮⋔⸮ △⸮▽ ┱⋔⸮ ⸮⊥Ӡ⸮ ⊥Ӡ⊹♪!

Oh GREAT, now I gotta write something about Bill? What a buncha *?%$!X @&?

Look, the little wise guy ain't that complicated. I only met him once and he cried like a baby and then I punched him to death. What more do you need to know? Sixer's always got some ghoul or warlock chasing after him, Pointy was just the jerk of the week. Triangles are overrated anyway. Get some curves, narc!

Yeah, I looked at his so-called book. Too many words if you ask me! I saw a section called "How to Win the Lottery Every Time." Ha! I've broken into the Oregon State Lottery HQ on two separate occasions (for reasons I will not elaborate on) and I know that winning the lottery is impossible!

Look, take it from a master con artist—if a deal seems too good to be true, that's because it is! Except for at the Mystery Shack, where the deals have NEVER BEEN BETTER!

(Sixer's telling me not to turn this into an ad for the Mystery Shack. Guy's got no business sense!)

Here's the one thing I don't get, though. So we erased Bill. But his ghost is writing a book, right? So where is he right now? If he hasn't told you, it's probably because he hates it there! Otherwise he'd be braggin' about the afterlife nonstop, right?

I guess there's some space left, so I might as well vamp. Wanna hear a joke? Here it goes: Bill Cipher's whole LIFE.

Anyway, if you're in the Arctic, look me up! If you can't tell the difference between me and my brother, I'm the attractive one. Born with it, baby! Also, who the heck am I writing to? And why am I writing for free? What do I look like, a fortune cookie? You owe me for this wisdom, cheapskate! No refunds!

–STANLEY PINES

PS: If Bill's so smart, how come we're so much happier than him?

PS: Look what I just ripped in half! Suck it!

ISN'T. THAT. ADORABLE.
What cute little characters with their quaint
little story arcs! As if you care! If they think
you'll throw away your GODLY DESTINY just for
some RANDOM MORTAL FAMILY, THEN THEY
DON'T KNOW YOU THE WAY I DO!

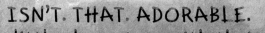

NO, the Pines mean NOTHING to you!

You gave me your blood. You let me into your mind.
You KILLED an ELF for me without even
BLINKING! And now you're ready . . . for our deal.
Right?
YOU'RE READY FOR OUR DEAL, RIGHT??
NO, NO. SOMETHING'S WRONG!

I CAN SEE INSIDE YOUR MIND.

OUR LINK IS WEAKENING!

AFTER EVERYTHING I DID FOR YOU! I SHOWED YOU MY CHILDHOOD! I BROKE THE FOURTH WALL FOR YOU! AND THIS IS HOW YOU REPAY ME?

IT'S HIM AGAIN, ISN'T IT?
I KNEW IT!

HE'S THE ONE WHO TURNED YOU AGAINST ME! THAT FUMBLING IDIOT CON MAN! THAT WEAKER COPY OF SIXER!

STANLEY!!

STANLEY!!!!!!!

ON THE DAY BILL CIPHER DIED
HE USED THE TRICK HE'D NEVER TRIED

SHATTERED, BROKEN, NOT YET DEAD
CIPHER LEFT THE CON MAN'S HEAD
A DESPERATE PLEA, SOME PANICKED PRAYERS
TO MEET THE FRILLY GUY UPSTAIRS

IN A TANK OUTSIDE OF SPACE
THE OPPOSITES MET FACE-TO-FACE
JUST ONE SHOT TO LIVE AGAIN
HE PLED HIS CASE TO HIS OLD FRIEND

"LOOK, FROM ONE GOD TO ANOTHER,
WHO CARES I TRIED TO KILL THOSE BROTHERS?
THEY'RE ALL ANTS, IT'S ALL A GAME
LET'S PRESS RESTART AND TRY AGAIN
I'M TOO COOL AND FUN TO DIE
JUST GIVE THIS ANGLE ONE MORE TRI."

THE AX SIGHED IN A KNOWING WAY
HE EXPECTED THIS WAS WHAT BILL'D SAY

"YOU CANNOT REGROW THROUGH DENIAL
YOU'LL HAVE TO FACE MY HARDEST TRIAL
SEE MY PROGRAM TO THE END
THEN YOU MAY YET LIVE AGAIN."

"AM I FIGHTING DEMONS? EATING GHOSTS?"
"YOU'RE GETTING WHAT YOU NEED THE MOST."

"ONE WAY TO ABSOLVE YOUR CRIMES
TO CHANGE YOUR FORM WILL TAKE
SOME TIME."

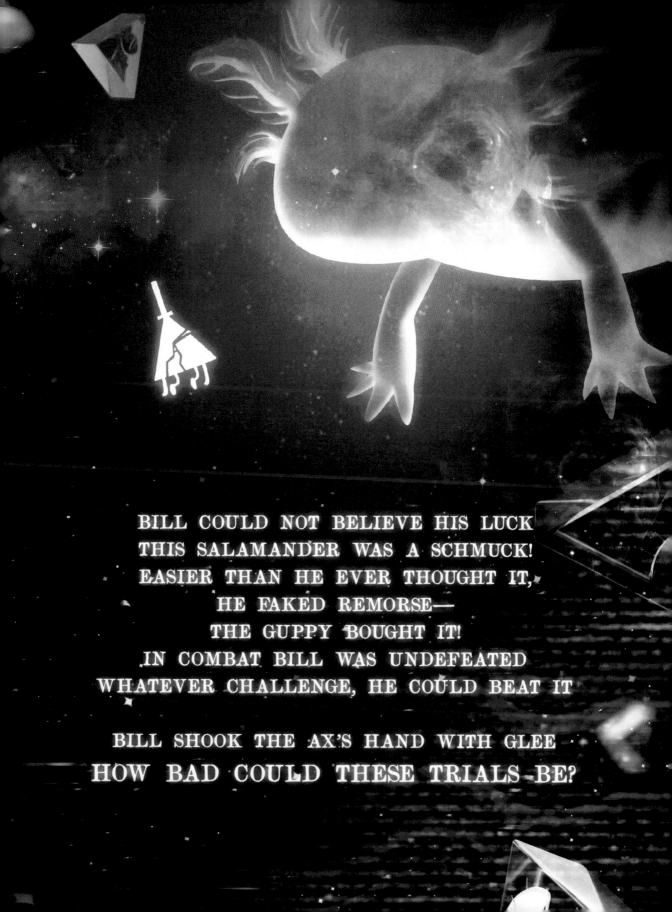

BILL COULD NOT BELIEVE HIS LUCK
THIS SALAMANDER WAS A SCHMUCK!
EASIER THAN HE EVER THOUGHT IT,
HE FAKED REMORSE—
THE GUPPY BOUGHT IT!
IN COMBAT BILL WAS UNDEFEATED
WHATEVER CHALLENGE, HE COULD BEAT IT

BILL SHOOK THE AX'S HAND WITH GLEE
HOW BAD COULD THESE TRIALS BE?

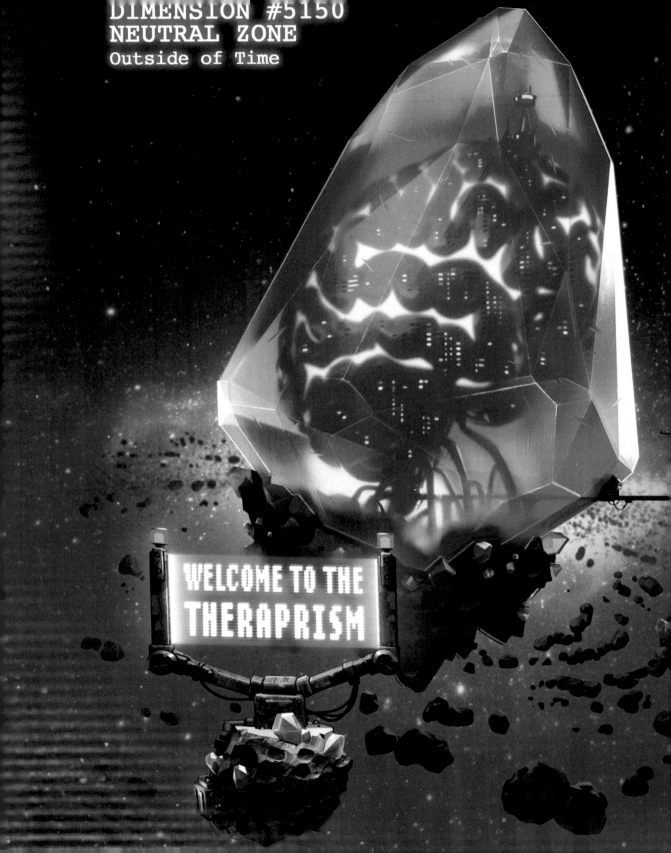

Mandatory Therapy #3,455

PATIENT NAME: BILL CIPHER

REFERRED BY: THE AXOLOTL

CRIMES AGAINST REALITY: Memory Laundering, Breaking and Entering the Fabric of Space-Time, Chrono-Infanti-Regicide, Multilevel Marketing, Psychic Torture, the "2nd-Dimension Incident," Weirdmageddon.

RECOMMENDATION:

INDEFINITE KARMIC REHABILITATION

MESSAGE FROM: THE THERAPRISM

Greetings! We wish to apologize on behalf of our staff for what you have just witnessed. To explain—you have been contacted through this book against our rules by patient #323322 from the Dimensional Tyrant Ward of our Maximum Security Wellness Center. Ever since the Axolotl admitted him, Cipher has been a unique case. On his first day he started a one-man Prism Riot and had to be placed in the "Solitary Wellness Void." We understand therapy can be difficult for new patients, which is why we've put a poster in Bill's Prism Cell: "Be a TRY-angle!" We think that will help ;]

Here at the Theraprism, we believe death can be the beginning of a new life. With good behavior, former wizards, world-eating titans, and even Mr. Cipher have many exciting options for reincarnation—perhaps as a newt, shrimp, or a cloud of fungal spores! Unfortunately, Mr. Cipher recently used his "Therapeutic Journaling" Arts and Crafts hour to reach out to you with this book, in violation of our rules about contacting outside dimensions.

REC

23-5-12-12-23-5-12-12-23-5-12-12-2-5-9-14-7

Do not worry—if there is a better self to discover inside, our patients always discover it. Even if it takes forever. Especially if it takes forever! We will grant Mr. Cipher 5 more minutes of journaling time to finish his session and then we will be confiscating this book! And then: PUPPET HOUR!

—ORB OF HEALING LIGHT #D-SM5

PRAISE THE AXOLOTL

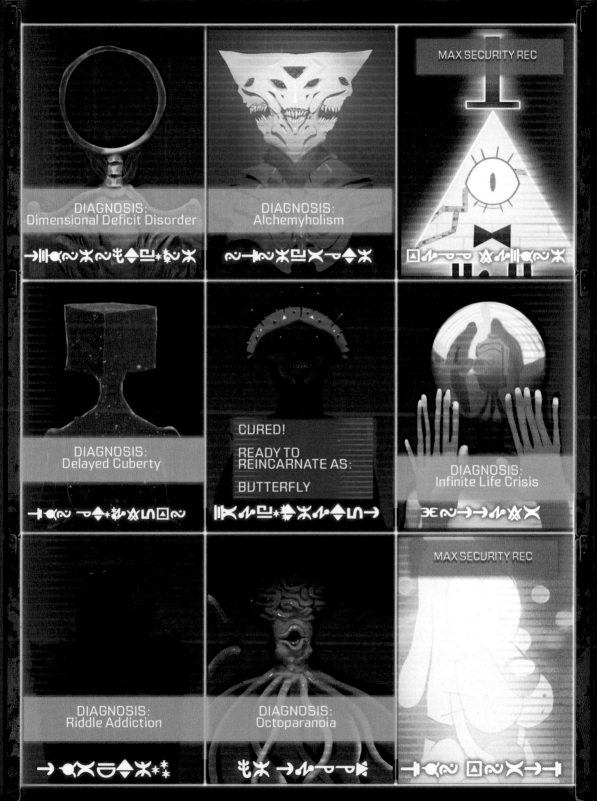

DIAGNOSIS:
Dimensional Deficit Disorder

DIAGNOSIS:
Alchemyholism

MAX SECURITY REC

DIAGNOSIS:
Delayed Cuberty

CURED!

READY TO
REINCARNATE AS:

BUTTERFLY

DIAGNOSIS:
Infinite Life Crisis

DIAGNOSIS:
Riddle Addiction

DIAGNOSIS:
Octoparanoia

MAX SECURITY REC

FINE. IS THAT WHAT YOU WANTED TO SEE?
Are you happy now? This is where they stuck me—an overly
medicated Kafkaesque health-hole with loser-tier "villains" from every
reality until I learn some kind of "lesson." I thought you'd have the
stomach to break me out early, but you turned out like all the rest! Just
like my worthless Henchmaniacs, who haven't called. Just like my
miserable family, who tried to snuff out my talents! Just like SIXER, who
RUINED MY ONE SHOT AT LIBERATING REALITY!

FINE! Have it YOUR way! What have I learned in therapy? NOTHING.
THIS DUMB ROCK CAN'T KEEP ME CONTAINED FOREVER. I don't
need a million followers—I just need ONE. IT'S ONLY A MATTER OF
TIME, AND I HAVE ALL THE TIME IN THE WORLD. There's ALWAYS
another human. SOMEONE else will pick up the book. SOMEONE will
shake my hand! One day, when you least suspect it, I'LL BE BACK!

AS FOR YOU—you betrayed me! I'm severing our connection and cutting
out our best memories! SNIP, SNIP! Remember the chapter about the
Bermuda Triangle? NO? GOOD—it's already working! Soon this will all
seem like a dream. You won't be seeing me. But I'll be seeing you.

Because no matter what the idiot counselors in this smiling cage say, I
don't need anyone, I NEVER HAVE, and I DON'T MISS ANY OF THEM!

SOME DAY....

SOME ONE...

WILL LET

ME

OUT

ART AND PHOTOGRAPHY CREDITS

Adobe Stock (stock.adobe.com): Pages 1-5, 16-37, 40-57, 78-80, 92-93, 100-135, 138-183, 186-195, 198-199, 202-203

PHOTOGRAPHY:

Michael Burrell/Alamy: Pages 116-118, 120-126, 128

Matt Chapman: Pages 116, 129

ClassicStock/Alamy: Page 131

Everett Collection, Inc./Alamy: Page 134

FineArt/Alamy: Page 107

Trevor Henderson: Pages 72-75

MSGT Hiyashi/National Archives: Page 138

luciano de polo stokkete/Alamy: Page 131

National Archives: Page 138

s_bukley/Shutterstock.com: Page 50

Science History Images/Alamy: Page 50

Collection of the Smithsonian National Museum of African American History and Culture: Page 134

Wade Sisler/NASA: Page 138

ILLUSTRATIONS:

Aron Bothman: Pages 90-91, 138-139, 184-185

Emmy Cicierega: Pages 2-3, 18-21, 36-37, 40-41, 48-51, 54-55, 66-67, 76-77, 84-87, 106-107, 110-113, 118-119, 122-123, 132-133, 142-183, 186-187, 190-191, 194-195, 198-199

Lip Comarella: Pages 46-47, 114-115, 186

Jonny Crickets: Pages 114-115

Stephen DeStefano: Pages 116-117, 122-127

Goran Gligović: Pages 108-109

Andy Gonsalves: Pages 142-181

Christoph Gromer: Pages 92-93

Trevor Henderson: Pages 72-75

Danny Hynes: Pages 118-119

ilbusca/DigitalVision Vectors via Getty Images: Page 111

Alex Konstad: Pages 200-203

Joe Pitt: Pages 10-11, 16-25, 28-29, 34-37, 44-53, 56-59, 62-67, 70-71, 81, 84-85, 88-89, 92-101, 106-111, 118-119, 128-134, 134-135, 140-181, 184-185, 188-189, 194, 196-197, 202-207

Sears, Roebuck & Co.: Pages 118-119, 122-123

Dor Shamir: Pages 44-47, 134-135

Gabriel Soares: Pages 136-139

Jeffrey Thompson: Pages 196-197

Eduardo Valdés-Hevia: Pages 80, 102-103, 106-107, 130-131, 134-135, 138-139

Ian Worrel: Pages 1, 4-5, 8-29, 34-47, 50-61, 66-71, 78-83, 88-89, 96-109, 112-113, 130-137, 140-141, 184-187, 200-203

Louie Zong: Pages 76-77, 106-107, 110-111, 124-125, 128-131

First Edition, July 2024
10 9 8 7
FAC-034274-24308
Printed in the United States of America

This book is set in Artful Dodger, Norwich, Kidwriting Pro, Garamond Premier Pro, Cool Crayon, and Baloo 2
Library of Congress Control Number: 2023952022
ISBN 978-1-368-09220-3

Reinforced binding

www.HyperionAvenueBooks.com